"That storm front is moving pretty fast. Head to the Gate House with the team. I'll call on the house phone when I need you. Give me an hour or two and then be ready to collect us."

"Very well, sir. Would you like us to inform her uncle where she is?"

"Yes. Tell him she's safe with me. That it was last-minute nerves and that we'll be returning to the castle by nightfall and married then." He hoped.

"Very well, sir. And...er...good luck with the princess."

Luck? That would have nothing to do with this. With San Nicolo at stake, he was prepared to use all the powers of persuasion he had to convince his little runaway that marriage to him would be all to her benefit.

A flurry of wind snatched up clouds of wild flower petals and swirled them at his feet like confetti.

He recrossed the threshold—still brideless.

For now, Leo thought.

Julieanne Howells loves the romance of a stormy day, which is just as well because she lives in rainy North East England. On inclement days, if she's not writing and reading, she has a fondness for cooking. Sometimes her efforts are even edible. She compensates for her lack of domestic skills by being an expert daydreamer, always imagining ways for plucky heroines to upend the world of handsome, provoking heroes. For Julieanne, writing for Harlequin is just about the perfect job.

Books by Julieanne Howells

Harlequin Presents

Desert Prince's Defiant Bride

Visit the Author Profile page
at Harlequin.com for more titles.

Julieanne Howells

STRANDED WITH HIS RUNAWAY BRIDE

HARLEQUIN
PRESENTS

ISBN-13: 978-1-335-58385-7

Stranded with His Runaway Bride

Harlequin Enterprises ULC
22 Adelaide St. West, 41st Floor
Toronto, Ontario M5H 4E3, Canada
www.Harlequin.com

Printed in U.S.A.

STRANDED WITH
HIS RUNAWAY BRIDE

CHAPTER ONE

THE CATHEDRAL OF St Peter's was looking its baroque best. Decked out in floral displays so spectacular they were upstaged only by the guests in all their wedding finery. Half the crowned heads of Europe were sitting in the congregation. Joined by presidents, prime ministers and, of course, all the senior officials of the principality of Grimentz. There to see its ruler wed.

So for His Serene Highness Prince Leopold Friedrich von Frohburg, waiting in the sacristy for proceedings to begin, his cousin's whispered message was not what he wanted to hear.

'It appears your blushing bride has fled.'

Leo swirled from the mirror where he'd been submitting to the last adjustments of his perfectionist valet.

'Although—' Seb added casually, and entirely at odds with the gravity of the situation '—it would be more accurate to say disappeared. Because one minute Princess Violetta was in her room at the castle and then, *poof...*' He snapped his fingers in the air for effect. 'Gone.'

Leo glared at his cousin. Prince Sebastien von Frohburg was the only person on the planet he truly trusted, which meant he allowed him informalities he'd tolerate from no one else. But this was definitely not the time for any of them.

'A young woman in her wedding dress, and wearing our priceless Elisabetha tiara, I might add, has simply vanished?'

Seb shrugged. 'That about sums it up, yes.'

'Who the hell allowed that to happen?'

His cousin slanted him a look. 'Er...well, that would be you, Leo, wouldn't it?'

Leo ignored the implication.

Get to know this one, Seb had begged him. *Woo her...don't take the chance.*

But he'd been reassured that this Della Torre sister was different. Biddable. Willing. Decorous. And certainly, at the few joint functions they'd attended, her hand had been cool and steady in his while she'd played the part of consort-to-be flawlessly.

Better than the last. The elder sister who'd run off with her bodyguard—a bodyguard!—a month before she was due to fulfil her decade-long engagement to marry him, a prince, and monarch of the oldest and richest principality in Europe. Where was the comparison?

The shame, of course, had all been attached to

her family. He and his father had made sure of it. No woman could be allowed to sully the great name of von Frohburg. Especially not a Della Torre one. They'd been a thorn in the side of the von Frohburgs for four hundred years.

Their grand duchy sat opposite Grimentz, separated by only a thin stretch of water. With no males to inherit, once Leo wed the female about to become the next grand duchess, her little state would rejoin his.

A bloodless reunification after centuries of bitter waiting.

For that prize Leo was ambitious enough to risk another go at marrying into the family. Despite the elder sister's rebellious streak.

Violetta, the younger daughter, her uncle and regent, had assured him, had been carefully raised and would never do such a thing.

No female had ever been allowed to rule the duchy in her own right, and none of the officials were keen to try that now. The Della Torres had approached his father fifteen years ago. Once it became clear the grand duke and his wife would have no male heir.

Leo hadn't seen the need to get to know the second daughter any better, other than at the handful of official functions they'd attended together as a betrothed couple. He'd gone through all the relevant groundwork when he'd been engaged to her sister. He knew the key players, the role she had in her duchy. Her uncle had been involved in the first negotiations anyway and he was still in place. It was essentially just a matter of replacing one sister with the other in the existing arrangements. All the requisite background checks revealed a female who'd led a quiet and blameless life.

Leo liked the fact she'd appeared bland and undemanding at their few meetings. It boded well for a businesslike union with no complications: like romantic expectations on the girl's part. Or, heaven help him, emotions. Life had long since taught him to be done with all that. While she wasn't a beauty like her sister, he was confident he'd be able to do his duty in bed and get the son and heir he needed. The future of his country and his people depended on him.

But could it be happening again? Was this girl eloping too? Anger and humiliation sliced through his gut.

'Was she alone?' Leo growled.

'As far as we know. It seems to be a spur-of-the-moment thing. There were less than ten minutes between her maids leaving and her uncle showing up to escort her here—' Seb paused to fish his phone from a pocket. 'Interesting. One of the businesses supplying flowers for the reception has reported a van stolen from the castle courtyard.'

'So now she has transport?'

'Looks that way. But where could she go? She's

hardly been here. How well could she know Grimentz?'

Barely at all. Historically, the two families had kept their distance since the treacherous Della Torres, then a vassal family, had stolen the grand duchy for themselves from his ancestors four centuries ago.

Unless she'd bribed a Grimentzian boatman to take her back across the water, there was only really one place she *could* go. The one place Leo knew for certain the girl had visited in Grimentz. Unfortunately, this was the last place he'd ever wanted to set eyes on again.

He began striding towards the private side entrance of the cathedral, the one shielded from the press and the crowds lining almost every other inch of the capital, calling for a car—a fast one— and issuing a rash of orders as he went. For his security chief. And for Seb, his best man, who, with the abrupt cessation of his other duties, was now in charge of damage limitation.

'The official line will be that she's taken ill,' Leo said as he strode 'The wedding is postponed. No bride wants her special day spoiled by a bout of the runs.'

Seb winced. 'You want everyone to think your absent bride is stuck in her bathroom? The press will have a field day.'

'Not my problem. That's hers. She ran away.

My protection is no longer a given,' Leo said, arriving at the doorway as a red Ferrari pulled up.

Seb's beloved car. Leo had indulged his cousin, who'd insisted he should surrender his bachelorhood in true playboy style, and allowed him to drive them both to the cathedral in it. The crowds had lapped it up. Cheering like maniacs as the groom and his best man climbed out.

Something more anonymous would have been his preference now, but at least the thing would eat up the miles between him and his missing bride. She'd had maybe a twenty-minute head start and if she was heading where he believed this would get him there before anyone else.

He climbed in.

'What do you want me to do with that lot back there?' Seb waved a hand in the direction of the cathedral behind them.

'You're supposed to be the charming one. I'm sure you'll work something out. And tell the staff in the castle they get a bonus for their silence. Any who do decide to talk to the press will not only lose their job, but get themselves and their family kicked out of the principality. Permanently.'

Seb looked shocked. 'Can we even do that?'

'We can now. Blame the woman. The shame all goes one way, remember.'

'So where precisely are you going?' Seb asked, leaning on the open door.

'Grandmother's chateau. Violetta went there

every summer. Right up to Grand-Mère's death four years ago.'

'But you had it closed up.'

'Which makes it even more perfect as a bolt-hole, don't you think?'

Seb's brow knotted. 'Wait, isn't that where—'

'Yes.' Leo cut him off. 'And I won't let that happen again.'

Leo lowered the car window to give some last-minute instructions. 'Give the archbishop the blue suite at the castle. He's fond of the bed in those rooms. I'll have the girl back here before midnight and he can marry us in the chapel. You can be a witness. No need for anything grander. Get a press release ready so we can announce the marriage in the morning.'

'You're that confident about persuading her to come back?'

'She's not her sister. It's probably just nerves. There are numerous benefits to being married to me. She just needs to see the sense of it.'

'Oh, I'd definitely open with that. She'll be putty in your hands.'

'Seb, we're so close to getting the grand duchy back I can almost taste it. I won't be denied that by some unreliable girl who can't see what's good for her.'

None of his ancestors had ever come this close to regaining the duchy. Not even his father. Leo would wed the Devil's mistress to prove to that cold-hearted bastard he was better than him and all their mutual ancestors put together.

He gunned the engine and sped out of the cathedral close, into the streets that had been closed for the duration of the wedding celebrations and kept clear for service vehicles. Heading north, out of the capital. Twenty miles to the very edge of his realm. Where Grimentz finally succumbed to the mountains and its neighbours beyond.

As he drove Lake Sérénité glittered below him. How ironic. A lake called serenity dividing two ruling families who'd battled each other to a stand then maintained a belligerent silence of deep mistrust for four centuries. This wedding was supposed to have put an end to all that.

Beyond Sérénité's calm waters sat the grand duchy of San Nicolo, lush and green with its superb vineyards and rolling pastures. It wasn't rich like Grimentz. It hadn't embraced the financial services that had given his principality unimaginable wealth and global influence. But it was soft and welcoming in a way that Grimentz, with its dour medieval castle and looming mountains, could never be.

His ancestors had struggled over their peaks finding a rocky outcrop on the western edge of the lake, where they'd built their castle. As forbidding and unforgiving as the mountains that soared behind, it rose from the shoreline to dominate everything for miles around. Previous princes had

tried to pretty it up with fairy-tale turrets and terraced pleasure gardens, but at its heart it remained
what it was: a fortress.

But there was no castle hewn from cold rock for
the Della Torres. They lived in Palladian elegance.
Princess Violetta's forebears had fallen in love
with the Renaissance and remade San Nicolo in
its image, gracious and refined. Tourists flocked
to its chocolate-box capital and pretty villages to
quaff the wine and gorge themselves on the cheese
and pastries it was famed for. Its subjects were
comfortable, though perhaps not content. Since
the death of Violetta's parents in a plane crash
three years ago, just months after the elopement
of her elder sister, there had been rumblings that
the Della Torre family were no longer fit to rule.
Her uncle, the regent while Violetta was not yet
of age, was unpopular and fuelling the dissent
with his rigid and old-fashioned governance. The
sooner Leo could step in and take power—in the
name of his wife, of course—the better.

He only had approximately thirteen hours to do
that. After that, things became more complicated.

On the stroke of midnight, in the reverse of a
Cinderella tale, his flighty bride turned twenty-
one and would no longer be just Princess Violetta of San Nicolo, subject to her uncle's rule,
but would be transformed into Her Serene Highness the Grand Duchess Violetta Della Torre, absolute monarch.

Some weird twist in the San Nicolo succession meant her husband couldn't take power until she was twenty-one. But take power he would. San Nicolo was old-fashioned that way. Never before allowing a woman to rule in her own right, and her uncle was determined that wouldn't happen now. Though if they'd married before now Leo would have had months of deferring to him. Obliged to be involved in the country's affairs but with no actual power.

Leo had solved the problem by arranging the marriage for the eve of the princess's birthday. No frustrating wait, forced to watch as her uncle wielded power—badly, he might add—and no legal complications. Because if they *weren't* married by the time the girl reached her majority there'd be a tortuous legal process to have him recognised as Head of State in place of his wife.

He gritted his teeth as he drove. All that stood between him and achieving his lifelong goal was an unsteady girl. What was she running away from? A life of privilege, and of ease. He'd shoulder all the responsibilities of monarch. She'd never have to raise a finger. Never have to make difficult choices.

'The girl has no aptitude for the work,' her uncle had told him. 'Better to have you at the helm.'

Leo was fine with that. Glad to have no interference from the Della Torres. What had they achieved with their picture-postcard duchy?

Cheese, wine and tourism. That was the extent of their ambition. Leaving the people trapped in an agrarian living museum. He'd be bringing them up to date.

Once he'd made Violetta his wife.

Briefly he pitied the girl. Her father was happy to give away the first daughter to an enemy. The uncle even happier to hand over the second. No chance for her to be Grand Duchess in her own right. Her father and uncle preferring to relinquish the duchy's sovereignty rather than have a female at the helm. What a family to have!

Then he recalled the packed cathedral, the spoiled banquet, the bunting, drooping in the July heat, and his sympathy deserted him.

He slammed the car into a higher gear and screamed down the road.

He hoped he'd guessed her destination correctly. This was his way. React swiftly. It had been drummed into him since birth.

'Never dither. Better to act, and act decisively. Indecision is for commoners, boy.' His father's mantra. He'd learned it well. Along with several others.

'Kindness is a weakness you cannot afford.'

'Compassion is for fools.'

'Love is a lie.'

'Women are for bed sport and offspring and otherwise not to be trusted.'

Pity his father hadn't had one for dealing with

being jilted, twice. By the same damn family. But Leo knew what he would have said.

Marry her, get a son by her and we finally have the duchy back.

Oh, I intend to, Papa.

In his life he'd never wanted anything more than to be the von Frohburg to finally regain the grand duchy. To prove to his father, even though he was long gone, that he deserved to be the prince he'd been born to be.

Once he had secured her, he'd paint it as wedding jitters, all eased and soothed by her handsome groom. He'd have photos released. Preferably of her gazing up at him, doe-eyed and adoring. The least she could do under the circumstances.

If he failed, not only would he lose the chance of regaining the duchy but, should he die without siring a son, Grimentz would suffer the rule of Max, Seb's older half-brother.

It was hard to imagine a man less suited to the task.

Devoid of his sibling's intelligence and loyalty, Max cared for only two things: himself and his pleasures. That was it. He was dedicated to a life of indolence and excess. The principality had not risen to the heights it had under the guidance of such men.

Leo wouldn't let that happen. He was thirty years old. The time had definitely come for him to wed.

And reclaim San Nicolo at last.

He met no one on the road. The entire population would be watching the wedding. Either at home or in the streets of the capital. In just twenty minutes he passed the gatehouse and entered the grounds of the estate of his grandmother's chateau. The very last place he'd thought to visit again. After she'd left it to him in her will, he'd ordered it be practically closed up. Except for authorising a monthly visit by a housekeeper, maid and groundsman to see to any repairs and keep the place watertight, he'd wanted nothing more to do with it.

Damn and blast the girl. Why did she have to go there of all places? With all of its bitter memories and mountains of regret. A place he'd vowed to never set foot in again.

Where he'd taken the elder Della Torre girl, his first fiancée.

Francesca was the beauty of the family. She'd inherited her mother's blue eyes and golden hair. Her mother's height and lithesome figure too. She'd charmed and flattered him and given no inkling she'd been using him to plot her escape.

'Let's go to your grandmother's chateau,' she'd said. 'The two of us, for a night away from everyone and their prying eyes.' He'd believed her. When she'd asked if they could wait so she'd come to him a virgin on their wedding night, he'd agreed and they'd gone to their separate beds.

Only for him to discover the next morning that she'd run off. A month later she was married to her ex-bodyguard. Going to the chateau with him had simply been a way for her to escape the watchful eyes of her father and the San Nicolo security team.

Leo's humiliation had been complete, and his father's rage and censure had been blistering. But he'd learned his lesson well. He'd never trust a woman again.

The last section of road climbed upwards to the chateau itself. The road had become rutted, the winters having taken their toll. So intent was he on his destination he missed the deep pothole. Sadly, the car did not. On a shudder and with a sickening grinding noise he came to an abrupt halt.

Leo flung the door wide and climbed out into the July heat. He'd be completing his journey on foot. With a curse he set off, sweating already in his wedding regalia.

The woman had better be at the end of this track.

Then the chateau appeared from behind the trees. Somewhere Grand-Mère had laughingly called the summer house but Chateau Elisabetha had three floors, nine guest bedrooms and a ballroom lined with mirrors and finely painted figures of dancing couples. An elegant white limestone chateau, nestled in its own valley with lush green foothills behind, extensive gardens on all sides and its own boathouse and jetty on the lake. His grandmother's summer residence. She and her husband had originally bought the place when their daughter had married the ruling prince and when she was widowed, his grandmother had spent every summer there to be close to her.

Leo hadn't expected the rush of memories as he approached. That it would look pretty much just as he'd remembered. Before he'd turned fourteen, and fate had taken a different turn and holidays with his grandmother had instantly ceased.

The gardens were a little more overgrown than Grand-Mère used to keep them, but even there she was a lover of nature, letting every kind of lost, loveless creature find a home—including him once—so she might have approved of the meadow of wildflowers that had taken over the lawns.

He could see her now. On that terrace, over-looking the lake. Drinking schnapps by candle-light and listening to Buena Vista Social Club. With her beloved rescue dogs by her side. Various mutts missing a leg or an ear, or with a broken doggy heart that she somehow fixed. All once unloved creatures, given the best of homes in this chateau.

Sometimes other guests had joined them. Like that last summer he'd spent there, when the grand-children of her best friend had been invited to the house for two weeks.

Girls. One so young and tiny he and Seb had

dubbed her *la fée*, the fairy. He remembered she'd followed him around like a puppy. To a thirteen-year-old boy a small girl had been beneath his dignity, and he'd found a way to chase her off.

Then came that last visit, three years ago. When the chateau was his. Left to him in his grand-mother's will.

The night he'd spent here with Francesca, the elder of those two girls.

What a debacle that had turned out to be.

But despite all that, it was still a house that held a touch of magic. It wound its way around him now.

He fought it off. Now was not the time for pointless sentiment. It had never served him well in the past and he didn't need it for what he was about to do.

The florist's van sat abandoned at the side of the building. A large sunhat, gauzy scarf and sun-glasses stuffed on the dash. Probably also stolen from the florist. That would explain how his bride had driven from the castle unchallenged. She'd disguised herself.

Leo strode on. His determination building with each step. He'd caught up with her. Now to put a stop to this nonsense and persuade her to return with him.

CHAPTER TWO

VIOLETTA HEARD THE roar of the high-powered engine, cutting through the quiet, then the abrupt, grinding stop followed by the slam of a car door.

She dropped the receiver back into its cradle. No time to wait for Luisa to pick up the phone now.

From the window she saw a glossy red sports car hunkered under the trees. But whoever had climbed out of it had already disappeared into a dip in the drive and was lost from view.

How had they found her so quickly?

She hurried to throw back a dust sheet and perched in the middle of a long, high-backed chaise. Hoping she looked thoroughly regal and unassailable. Knowing if she stood, her trembling would show her to be the exact opposite.

Her heart pounding, she waited.

First came the crunch of booted feet on gravel.

Then the heavy strike of leather soles on the flagstones of the hallway.

She straightened her spine and stared resolutely

ahead. Whoever had come for her, she was determined she would not be going back with them. Then in *he* walked, and she fought to hide her shock. Never expecting that her forbidding groom would bother to come after her himself.

Violetta stared at the man filling the doorway. The man her sister had exiled herself to avoid marrying. How had Francesca described him? Like a half-tamed wolf: prowling, watchful and ever hungry. That was exactly the man who stood there now.

He was tall. He certainly always towered over her. Six feet two, she'd been told, when they'd determined what height heels she'd be permitted to wear at joint functions. At least three inches. Elevating her diminutive five feet two to the optimum height. The delicate bride to his alpha male prince, making the photos of the two of them together look perfect.

Unlike the match itself.

His dark hair, cut short at the sides, fell thick and lustrous across his forehead. There was a long, straight imperious nose—of course, what other kind would he have?—and deep-set blue eyes that women the world over swooned for.

Those eyes watched her now. His mouth might be smiling but, oh, those stunning eyes…they were scorching the flesh from her bones.

Feeling a sharp pull of attraction was deeply inconvenient though she should have expected it.

She'd not been immune to him on those few occasions they'd met. But the pulse of heat and longing had lasted only while she was in his company and any after-effects had been bested.

Eventually.

Violetta decided that right now her best defence against that was attack.

'Oh, it's you,' she said, as nonchalantly as she could, and in her native Italian, not his French that they'd always conversed in before. Hoping to insult him. That the man accustomed to a lifetime of deference had rarely been greeted with less.

But he countered all that with a gracious smile, and said, in the most perfect Italian accent that shivered over skin, 'You were expecting someone else?'

'My money was on it being the prime minister. When I heard the sports car, of course, I knew it wasn't him. Far too flashy and undignified.'

A strong male jaw tightened. He wasn't smiling quite so hard now.

'But I really wasn't expecting you. I thought you'd have been too busy.'

'My other appointments for the day were all cancelled. At rather short notice,' he added pleasantly enough. But she wasn't fooled. She could see the anger in the set of his shoulders and the fists bunched at his sides.

'Yeah, sorry about that...' She peered past him to the empty hallway.

'I'm here alone, if you're wondering. I took off so fast my security team didn't have time to follow. I told them I'd call them en route but, sadly, I forgot I'd left the valet in charge of my phone so they've no idea where I am.'

His crack security team did not have a clue where their prince was? That sounded unlikely. 'Won't they be out scouring the countryside for you?'

'Of course. But I doubt anyone will think to come here just yet.'

'You did.'

'But I know you have history with the place. As far as anyone else will recollect, you do not. Unless your uncle or your people consider it.'

She snorted. '*My* people have all been replaced and my uncle will hardly have cared about any holidays his niece once took.'

His brow knotted. 'Your people were replaced?' His surprise almost sounded genuine. But he'd had a hand in the changes to her team. She'd bet her life on it.

The man who stood before her now was palpably angry. Gone was the smoothly charming prince. Here was a creature of hard angles and bunched muscle. Was he bigger than she remembered? Surely not? It had only been two weeks since she'd last been in his company. Heat coursed through her belly.

She looked away to gaze straight ahead. Feigning aloofness, because inside she quailed. It gave her a moment to gather her wits. To push back the clamour of need.

Finally she steeled herself to it. Straightened her spine and met his eye.

His hard gaze burned into her. Not as a man wanted a woman but as a man wanted a thing, because to him she meant nothing more than a conduit to San Nicolo. Like every man in her life. Her only value to them was in the possessions she held. That was why it was him that followed her. She'd denied him the duchy and he was here to collect.

'I won't go back with you if that's why you're here?' she said, using French now.

She'd known this moment was coming but she hadn't expected to be completely alone with him when it did. And with him looking like *that*.

Stunning in full military uniform as Colonel-in-Chief of the Grimentzian Guards. With the addition of a blue sash denoting his royalty and his chest bristling with honours, her every soft feminine instinct wanted to simply drink in the sight.

Foolish woman. Think of something else.

Her gaze flickered over the bar of medals he wore. Apart from being born into privilege, the only child of a very important man, what single useful or arduous thing had he done to earn even one? By contrast she'd been denied every one of her own San Nicolo royal honours.

'It will be a mark of respect for your new po-sition as Crown Princess of Grimentz,' her uncle had said. Brushing aside her concerns, just as he had her team of faithful retainers, fired, moved on, or replaced over the last six months. Her chauffeur and Rolfe, her secretary, even Luisa, her dresser, her confidante, her friend. The one person she'd truly had to talk to. She'd been removed a week before this sham of a wedding. All with the agree-ment of her future husband, she had no doubt.

She couldn't think of any of that right now. She had to get through the next thirteen hours with-out succumbing to the faux charms of her groom and remain unwed. At one minute past midnight, she'd become Grand Duchess and no man would have any say in her life again.

'May I sit?'

She started. How could she have become so lost in her thoughts with him standing there?

The palm he ran over his face was the first sign of vulnerability she'd ever witnessed in his com-pany, and now she noticed the sheen of sweat on his forehead. He'd marched the last five hundred metres up that bank, in heavy military uniform and full summer heat. It was tempting to leave him where he stood but she was not a vindictive woman. She shuffled sideways, making room for him on her chaise.

As he prowled towards her Violetta wondered had she just invited a stalking tiger to come closer.

For heaven's sake, Violetta, make up your mind. Is he a wolf or a tiger?

With a click of his heels and a brief bow he sank down beside her. As his large frame lowered and his long legs folded beneath him, she decided he was a mix of both and all of him dangerous.

This close up he smelled amazing. But then he always did. It had taken at last twenty-four hours each time they'd met to expunge the effects of him from her consciousness.

A large and rather beautiful hand rested on his knee. The gleam of the ruby in his signet ring reminding her of another ring she should be wearing about now.

But here they were instead. Decked out in all their wedding regalia, perched together in this abandoned house of dust covers and long-ago laughter. The image, a stylist's dream. And a publicist's nightmare.

But as a portrait of a couple, it was quite fitting. The space between them a physical reminder of emotional ties between them. As in, there weren't any.

Violetta shot her former groom a sideways glance. There was an uncharacteristic weariness to the set of his shoulders and, she noted, a tiny nick on his jaw. As if the hand usually adept at the task had not been so steady shaving this morning.

She sent her gaze front and centre.

It really wouldn't do to dwell on anything so intimate as this man's toilette, or that he might have been nervous and that he had any vulnerabilities. That could lead to a host of other, less innocent and more dangerous thoughts.

What was he really but another in a series of powerful men who saw her as a commodity to be bartered? No different from her father or uncle. She despised each of them and this prince most of all because he was ready to marry a woman he barely knew, the sister of a woman who'd very publicly jilted him, to get his hands on the grand duchy. What a mercenary act.

And yet he called to her in some deep, dark, sensuous way. His presence throbbing through her like a heartbeat.

Needing to put some space between them again, Violetta stood and walked to the window. Beyond the gravel driveway the once immaculate lawns were lost beneath a riot of wildflowers. Uninvited, still they'd made it a refuge. Rather like her, fleeing to one of the few places she'd ever been happy, shown any genuine love. Her grandmother and Leo's had been bosom friends and every summer, even though their grandmother had been long gone, she and her sister had visited for a holiday. The only place in Grimentz she'd been permitted to see.

Grimentz. It had loomed over her, physically and emotionally, throughout her life. Every San Nicoloan knew that Grimentzian eyes turned covetously towards their lush pastures and elegant architecture.

But her uncle had decided that the time for the old animosities was over.

And her marriage was to be the means to that end.

Leo watched as his bride paced restlessly, as if even in this empty house she felt confined. Her trailing skirt sent up blooms of dust from the neglected floor.

She was small and slender with the dark hair and the brown eyes of her people. Certainly no beauty, but she had a warmth to her that could draw the eye; if you had the time or inclination to look.

She turned to him, instantly spoiling the effect. Her delicate heart-shaped chin had a mulish turn to it. It angered him. He had every right to expect nervous and abject apologies, not this hostility.

'Do you know when Marie Antoinette arrived in France for her wedding, they'd erected a tent that exactly straggled the border,' she said. 'They took her in there, stripped her of everything she wore and replaced each item so when she stepped onto French soil, she was dressed head to toe with French-made items. Even down to her underwear. As if they were trying to expunge what she was, as if it wasn't good enough.'

He experienced a faint sense of alarm. Had his people done something similar without his knowledge? No, surely not! He'd had approval of everything, including that dress.

The closely fitted, high-necked bodice and long sleeves were made of the finest ivory lace. A silk cummerbund circled her slender waist and beneath that a full skirt of plain ivory silk fell to the floor to cover her toes.

It pleased him, as it might any man in his position. The perfect, virginal bride in a gown fit for the princess consort she was meant to be.

'The dress, I think, is rather beautiful,' he said. Adding, for good measure, 'You look very lovely in it.'

'You don't have to wear it. And it's not me. It's not close to being me.'

His brow knotted. 'Then why, may I ask, did you choose it?'

'I didn't. You did.'

When he looked blankly at her she added, 'The photographs? The ones they sent for your approval. I quote.' She dropped her voice into a parody of his. '"Very nice, although of course she'll be wearing the Elisabetha tiara."'

He wasn't flattered by her impression. He assumed he wasn't meant to be. His anger spiked.

'You ran away because you don't like your dress?'

She shot him an angry look. 'If I'd been allowed the privilege of wearing a watch, I'd mark the time for posterity. Because that, Your Serene Highness, is the very first time you've asked me anything about how I'm feeling about our marriage.'

'Surely not. We've spoken numerous times.'

She gazed steadily at him and gave him the time to mentally run through their half-dozen encounters. All official functions. All surrounded by others. Okay, barely a genuine private moment.

'You asked me about the duchy's wine harvest,' she said. 'You asked me if I preferred the operas of Beethoven or Mozart.'

'Mozart.' He distinctly remembered that.

'Actually, I loathe opera. My parents were forever dragging me to it. So I lied.'

'You could have told me the truth.'

'What was the point? Would anything have made you change your mind about our marriage? Not with the grand duchy at stake.

'And you never gave the impression you cared either way about me. When you took my hand you could have been picking up a sock you were about to put on. You were that disengaged. It felt like you never really saw me. Do you know how demeaning that is? To be so…so…' she grappled for the word '…inconsequential.'

'But I remember a number of interesting conversations,' he said with a placating smile.

'Oh, yes, our…' she made quotation marks in the air '…"conversations". The first time we met, you granted me twenty minutes. We walked on the terrace at the castle. You pointed out the architecture and the modifications various forebears had made and those you were planning. Then you told me what would be expected of me as your wife. I forget the details but quiet compliance seemed to be the main requirement. And an heir or two, of course.

'After that we met ten minutes before appearing in public. Always in Grimentz. I was given details of where to stand, where to sit, when to sit. Definitely never before you were seated. Your staff had already sent over details of whom I might speak to, and what I should say, whom I would not be permitted to speak to. You were very clear on the topics of conversation. The wine harvest and cheese production of the principality. Any charities I was involved with, though nothing controversial, which precluded discussing the teenage mothers I support and get through school. You held my hand only when there were others around to see. By others, I mean other dignitaries or the press, not our own people. You never once called me by my given name or invited me to call you by yours. And after all that, you thought I'd relish the prospect of being married to you and be expected to have…to do…' she waved a hand through the air '…*that*. Should I go on?'

She made it all sound pretty damning. 'The walk on the terrace wasn't the first time we met,' Leo pointed out, trying to defend the indefensible.

She snorted. 'You behaved even worse on that

holiday we shared here. Because mostly you ignored me. When you did notice me, it was only to chase me with a handful of spiders. And I hate spiders,' she said, darkly.

He glanced to the shrouded light above her head where several cobwebs hung. She'd fled to the wrong house, then.

'I was thirteen. Perhaps you could allow I've matured since then.'

'Maturity and charm are not the same thing.'

Ouch.

'Then I beg your pardon, firstly for chasing you with spiders and latterly for apparently being a dolt of a fiancé.'

Her eyes widened. Perhaps she was not expecting the self-recrimination. But then her face crumpled. 'And what if we are physically incompatible? What if the sex were terrible? What if I didn't like it?' She sounded lost.

'Then I'd definitely be doing something wrong and I'm not known for that.'

She scowled at him. 'Of course, you've been allowed to have lots of experience. While I've had none. How is that fair? I've been protected so much I wouldn't know an erect penis from a bedpost. Not literally, of course. I've seen the pictures.'

Pictures? What sort of pictures? Arty ones? Erotic ones? His mind reeled.

'They didn't tell me you were so forthright.'

'I'm not. I'm normally very well behaved and ladylike. You must bring out the worst in me.'

She was pacing and muttering to herself. 'How did I let this happen? What was I thinking? Oh, and he just had to find me here, didn't he?'

His involvement in the conversation no longer seemed to be required. Much like his involvement as groom. At his own wedding.

The clock was ticking. He needed to control the situation. Calm her, charm her, persuade her back to the castle with him and get them married. Before midnight.

It was time to take a different tack.

'What were you going to do when you got here?' he asked.

Violetta stopped pacing.

Call Luisa from the house phone and have a boat sent along Lake Sérénité to collect her from the chateau's private jetty. But Luisa hadn't picked up the call and then the Ferrari had arrived.

'I don't know. I hadn't thought that far ahead. I suppose I'd hoped there would be a housekeeper or someone.' Lies, of course. She wasn't going to tell him, a powerful, self-interested man, what she ultimately hoped to do. She'd learned long ago to hold all her opinions close to her chest.

'You'd be lucky. The place has been closed up since my grandmother died.'

She looked around at the dust covers shrouding all the furniture.

'I can see that now. I was very sorry about her, by the way. I loved your grandmother.'

He didn't answer. Just stared at the floor between his knees. It was well known that grandmother and grandson had been estranged since he'd been a teenager. She wondered if Leo the man regretted that.

He looked up but made no comment. Apparently unmoved.

'We might be here for a while. This won't be the first place they'll think to look for us,' he said. 'In the meantime I think we should get more comfortable.'

Violetta's hand fluttered to her throat. He couldn't mean…

He raised a brow. 'I'd like to take off all this paraphernalia.' He gestured to his jacket and sash. 'This house may have many charms, but air conditioning isn't one of them.'

He stood, his fingers going to the bar of medals adorning his chest, but he struggled with the pin holding the rack in place. 'My apologies, but this appears to be stuck. I may need your help.'

Even though removing his jacket was a sign that he meant them to stay at least for a while—eating up a few more hours to midnight—could she risk getting closer to him? Actually touch him? Violetta's heart pounded at the thought.

'I won't bite, if that's what's concerning you,' he said, with a lopsided smile that made her heart beat even faster.

No, but she was concerned she might *want* him to. Why did her body have to react to him like this every time?

She stayed exactly where she was. 'Can't you just rip it off?' she said.

He looked appalled.

'One does not simply rip items from a Grimentzian Guards uniform. Besides, have you met my valet? If this goes back to Matteo anything less than pristine, he'll torment me for a month at least. Sending me off to official functions in a straw boater and lederhosen, or some such, and his reputation be damned.'

That made her smile despite herself.

She had met the valet. A trim, fifty-year-old. Half Scottish, half Italian and one hundred per cent forged in the grand houses of Europe. A gentleman's gentleman of such impeccable credentials and exacting standards it was he that chose his employer, not the other way round. The prince was not even the most elevated he'd served. Only one man met with his sartorial approval. The second most infamous playboy in Europe, Prince Sebastien von Frohburg.

The most infamous stood before her now. At least he used to be. Until his father died and, abruptly, he switched from party animal to serious and stern ruling prince. Up to then there'd been a stream of glamorous women in his past. All tall and blond and beautiful. Like her sister.

Quite the opposite of her.

Violetta's smile faded. Well, what did that matter? She didn't need to match up to any of them. She and the prince would be nothing to each other after today. She only had to get through the next few hours in his company.

She couldn't really say no to his request. Leaving him trussed up in that heavy, braided thing when indeed it was hot in here.

She swished her skirts, straightened her back then approached him. That seemed to amuse him. A distracting, crooked smile made an appearance.

This close up, her eyes were level with his broad chest, made still more impressive by the medals and starburst honours pinned to it.

Violetta's hand floated up to the medal bar that held the jingling rack of honours. Suspiciously, the pin came away easily. She carefully placed the bar on the chaise behind them. His intense blue eyes watched her every move.

'Don't do that.'

'Do what?' he asked, all innocence.

'Stare at me like that.' It was making her hot, much hotter than she already was in this tight-fitting, heavy-skirted dress.

'You said I'd never properly seen you before. I'm making up for it. I'll stop if it's making you uncomfortable.' His gaze lifted to fix on the room behind her. 'Is that better?'

She missed those blue eyes on her, but hell would freeze over before she'd admit to it. She reached for the sash traversing his chest, her hands caught the edge then lifted upwards. He dipped his head allowing her to lift it from him. Her wrist brushed the top of his hair. Soft and silken and feeling so ridiculously intimate.

She was being foolish. It was just hair, but her fingers trembled as she carefully placed the sash with the medals.

He sighed in relief as he slipped the jacket from his shoulders. The scent of his cologne and sweat filled the air. Violetta dipped her head, but still it invaded her senses.

'Thank you,' he said, undoing the top buttons on his collarless white shirt, rolling back his shirt sleeves.

Violetta blinked.

In full uniform he'd looked dashing, too handsome. Now, in braces and black trousers with the narrow scarlet stripe down the side, with rolled-back sleeves and part-unbuttoned shirt, he was gorgeous.

A flicker of movement from the gardens snapped her attention away.

'There's someone out there.'

Leo was instantly on guard, swinging round to place himself between her and the window.

Oh, chivalry!

Protected only by those paid to do so, and never truly valued by her family. Genuine chivalry had been in short supply in Violetta's life. How nice to experience it from this big, vital, handsome man. Her heart gave a most annoying squeeze.

'Where?' he demanded.

'In the treeline. Just beyond the wildflowers on the lawn.'

His eyes narrowed. 'I see nothing.'

'Maybe you were followed here after all.'

'Unlikely. Only my team saw me leave the cathedral and if anyone else had spotted me in the city they'd have assumed I was simply a guardsman tasked with returning the Ferrari to the castle.'

'Maybe there was someone already here when we arrived? A burglar or someone. Shouldn't we at least go and investigate?'

'If it makes you feel better I'll go and check. Wait here.' He started for the door. Violetta followed him.

'I'm not staying in here by myself. What if there's an accomplice already in the house?'

He looked down at her. 'Was the place locked when you arrived?'

'Yes, I retrieved the spare keys from the key safe where your grandmother kept them.'

'And all the shutters were still closed?'

'Yes, I opened this one so I had light in the room.'

'Well, then. How did this mysterious accomplice get into the house? Down the chimney?'

But she stared stubbornly back.

He sighed. 'Very well, Grand Duchessa, we'll go and check together.'

Leo exited the front door with Violetta trotting at his heels. As they approached the tangle of wildflowers on the lawn he hoped whichever of his security team she'd seen had made themselves scarce. If they hadn't, and she spotted them, they'd worked their last day for him. If it was paparazzi and they'd been allowed to penetrate the tight ring of security he'd ordered thrown around this place, years of loyal service or not, his head of security would also find himself out of a job.

He wanted her to believe they were entirely alone. He didn't want her thinking she could just march out of here and request help from one of his men. Not until he'd had time to talk her round and persuade her to marry him after all.

'Wait here,' he ordered as they reached the edge of the overgrown lawns.

Of course she ignored him. She hitched up her dress and clambered onto the lawn. Instantly struggling to wade through the tussocks of grass in heels and all those petticoats. She nearly tumbled and made a grab for his hand.

Irritated, he took it, his own progress slowed by

having to assist her with almost every step. Eventually they reached the treeline.

The tall grass swayed in the breeze. The boughs creaked in the heat. A startled bird shot for the safety of the skies. Otherwise, silence.

'See,' he said, 'no one here at all.'

She peered around him. 'The grass is battered down and there is a trail leading away from it.'

Damn it, she was smarter than he'd been told. Willing and decorous—the penis and bedpost remark came back to mind—neither of those had been true so far.

'A deer, most probably. Basking. It took off when it heard us,' he said.

She snorted. 'Sharks bask. Deer maybe sun themselves. But that…' she pointed at the bowl of flattened grass '…is far too big to have been made by a deer.'

He pretended to assess the terrain, squinting at the mountains behind them. 'I suppose we're high enough up for it to have been a wolf.'

'A wolf?' She shrieked, flattening herself against his back.

'Relax, it'll be long gone. It would have run off the moment we stepped outside.' He looked down at her. 'Satisfied?'

She sent one last piercing glance to the trees but there was nothing to see. 'I suppose it could have been a bird.'

She struggled to turn to walk back to the house.

In frustration Leo scooped her up and hefted her over the grass to the gravel drive.

As he picked his way back through the tussocks of flowers she clung to his neck. Her hips and thighs were swathed by all her petticoats. But her waist was slender and her arms supple. Small breasts pressed against his chest.

What would she do if he carried his prim bride right over the threshold back into the house? With all the connotations that had.

His foot landed on the first of the gravel.

'Put me down. I can walk from here.'

'It's only a few more paces to the house.'

'You are not carrying me over the threshold. Put me down. Now!'

Biddable? Strike that too.

'As you command, Grand Duchessa,' he purred.

'Stop calling me that. I'm not the grand duchess until midnight.'

Wasn't he acutely aware of that?

The second her dainty feet hit the ground she scooted away from him, making a production of shaking out her petticoats and smoothing down the skirt. Beautifying the dress that she apparently loathed. She gave a little sniff of derision and stalked off towards the house, voluminous skirt dragging through the gravel. Her maids would never get the dirt out of it, he thought.

Leo strolled in her wake. Oddly fascinated by the angry sway of her hips in that full gown. What were her legs like beneath all that fabric? Long? Slender? Would there be a supple curve to her thighs? He'd never wondered before and during their previous meetings they'd both been in evening wear, which had meant full-length gowns for her.

Her sister too had been lithe. She'd been a keen rider. Did Violetta share that passion? He was beginning to realise how little he actually knew of his intended. And that it might be useful to know more if he was going to change her mind about marriage.

The midday sunshine glinted in her hair as she walked away. He'd only ever seen her hair styled in an elaborate chignon. Much as it was now. Were those rich brown locks as plentiful as they appeared or was the bounty of intricate coils helped along by a hairpiece? If it was all her own, would it spill to her waist? Long enough for a man to wind his hands through?

Leo frowned. Surprised by the direction of his thoughts, he dismissed them. It was probably the novelty of finding his chaste bride was not as meek as he'd thought.

A nearby bush interrupted his musings.

'Sorry, sir,' it hissed.

Leo halted. 'I think we got away with it,' he answered, his voice low as Violetta disappeared into the house.

He squinted at the horizon in earnest. An ominous cloud had appeared over the mountains to the north. Bad weather had been forecast but not until later in the day. Contingency plans had been made to take the wedding reception from the gardens and inside the castle when necessary.

'That storm front is moving pretty fast. Head to the gatehouse with the team. Anyone coming to the valley will have to come past you there anyway, so we should be safe enough. I'll call on the house phone when I need you. Give me an hour or two and then be ready to collect us.'

'Very well, sir.'

The bush rustled as the guard began crawling away.

'Wait. Check on something, find out what happened to the princess's people. She said they'd been dismissed. Find out where they are and have them brought to the castle'

'We'll get on it straight away. Would you like us to inform her uncle where she is?'

'Yes. Tell him she's safe with me. That it was last-minute nerves and that we'll be returning to the castle by nightfall and we'll be married then.'

He hoped.

'Very well, sir. And…er…good luck with the princess.'

Luck? That would have nothing to do with this. With San Nicolo at stake, he was prepared to use all the powers of persuasion he had to convince his little runaway that marriage to him would be all to her benefit.

A flurry of wind snatched up clouds of wild-flower petals and swirled them at his feet, like so much confetti.

He recrossed the threshold—still brideless.

For now, Leo thought.

CHAPTER THREE

THE SALON WAS DESERTED, so Leo paused only to collect his discarded jacket, sash and medals bar.

At the rear of the hallway, tucked beneath the grand staircase, the door to the service areas stood ajar.

He found her in the vast kitchen.

The staff who visited the chateau every four weeks kept them spotless. It smelled of beeswax, much as it always had. The long table and rustic chairs gleamed with it, as did the enormous oak dresser that still sat against the wall facing the large window. The granite worktop and the old range cooker were polished to a shine.

He knew this kitchen well. His grandmother loved to cook and often he and Seb would sit with her while she chopped this, stirred that.

It was a house where a royal heir had got to live a life as close to normal as possible. He and Seb were allowed to play outside all day, coming home filthy and starving, to plates piled with fresh pasta and the best tomato sauce he'd tasted to this day. Allowed to bathe after eating with no one nagging him about correct manners. Allowed to get up from the table and collect whatever he wanted from the pantry. To wind his arms around Grand-Mère's neck and listen to her tell fascinating tales of her youth with her best friend, Violetta's grandmother. To go to bed when he was tired and to speak when he had something to say and be listened to.

He glanced around.

His grandmother's battered old CD-player still sat on the oak dresser and beside it a small stack of CDs. Perhaps when the staff had cleared the house, they hadn't realised it was a personal item of the former and kept it to use themselves.

Violetta had found a glass and filled it with water from the tap. She gulped it down in one go then wiped her mouth with the back of her hand.

In that grand dress, fit for the princess she was, and with the emerald-strewn Elisabetha tiara on her head, it was yet another incongruous picture from today.

She shook the empty glass at him. 'Would you like one?'

'Please.'

He hung his jacket and sash on a chair back and placed the medal bar on the table while she hunted out a second glass and filled it from the tap. Before she could set it on the table, he reached out to take it from her hand, making a point of brushing her fingers. Her little shudder pleased him.

She stepped back and folded her arms across her chest.

'What do you think is happening back in the capital?'

'They've been told the wedding is postponed because the bride is indisposed. Stuck in her bathroom.'

Her eyes flew wide. 'You told them *what*? I'll never live that down!'

'Whereas jilting your groom will cover you in glory?'

She lifted her chin. 'There's something romantic and noble about fleeing from an unwanted wedding.'

'Not when you're the one left dealing with the fallout.'

'So what happens now?' she asked.

He sat. Draped an arm along the back of the seat next to him, crossed one long leg over the other. Relaxed and apparently unconcerned that a congregation packed with high-born guests and dignitaries waited on his pleasure in St Peter's cathedral.

He took a long, slow drink of his water and watched as Violetta swallowed convulsively.

'What would you like to happen?' he said.

'You expect me to believe that what I want will

really matter in the long run? No man has ever cared about what I want.'

'I assure you, *this* man has the most acute interest in what you want right now.'

She studied him. Saying nothing as she collected his empty glass, rinsed and dried it and returned it to the cupboard.

She squared her shoulders, a gesture he was coming to recognise as her plucking up her courage, and turned to face him.

'Perhaps this wouldn't have happened if we'd got to know each other a little better. Maybe we could do that now? What I've really wanted is the chance to get to know you better.'

Uh-oh. He'd heard that before. Usually from a woman when she wanted to cling and he didn't do clingy. He didn't do getting to know anyone better. That wasn't his way, not any more.

Once they were safely wed, he'd make it clear that a cosy intimacy wouldn't be high on his list of priorities.

Certain she wasn't being honest with him and wanting to probe for the truth, he asked, 'Would there be any point if we're not getting married?'

'Maybe you could, you know…change my mind?'

Another lie. Why didn't she just ask to be taken home? It was obvious she was stalling, but to what end?

For now, he'd go along with her. He studied the

small pert breasts, the neat waist, and the maidenly flush creeping across her cheeks.

'You won't do it like that.' Her hand was back at her throat. 'I'm not about to be seduced by your charms. Because so far, I've yet to see any.'

He shouldn't have been insulted but her blunt dismissal of him as an adult, sexual being was offensive.

'You haven't seen any because I've yet to use them. Once I do, you'll be thinking differently.'

Her mouth tightened. 'So sure of your own worth. But you forget, unlike all your other conquests I'm not impressed by your title and your wealth. I have enough of those of my own. And on those few occasions we did meet, you were so self-absorbed how could I believe you'd really mean any of it now?'

His gut twisted on a rare moment of shame. Hadn't he been on the receiving end of just that kind of behaviour himself in the past? From his father. He shared the man's genes but that was where he wanted all similarities to end.

She'd drifted to his jacket hanging over the chair back and was studying the insignia still attached. She reached out to stroke the gold badge, shaped in a pair of wings, that had been pinned to his right breast.

'What's this?'

'A French Army Parachute qualification.'

She glanced up. 'An honorary award, I pre-sume?'

'Certainly not.'

'You actually took the course? Isn't it extremely tough?'

'Yes. Achieving that nearly broke me.'

She flashed him a look that suggested she wished it had.

'And this?' She trailed a finger across a second badge that had sat just left of his heart, and a frisson of something skittered through him. He shifted his shoulders.

'Helicopter pilot's badge.'

He waited for her to be impressed.

She tapped at the pilot's badge. 'I wonder how good you are at this…' her fingers turned back to the parachute wings '…if you also need these.'

The little madam.

'The altitude is often too low for a parachute to have worked.'

That wasn't true but she wouldn't know that and for some reason he wanted her to be impressed with him.

She wasn't.

'So you don't have a head for heights?'

'Flinging myself from a perfectly good aero-plane with essentially a large tablecloth strapped to my back would suggest otherwise.'

But he noticed her lips curling into a smile.

She'd been teasing him and suddenly he wasn't half as annoyed about that as he might have been.

Flirting? This was progress.

If his little *grand duchessa* wanted to play, bring it on. He was a master.

'And what, might I ask, have you ever done to drive terror into your bones?' he teased right back.

Instantly her face fell and the good humour evaporated. 'Allow myself to be put in this dress with no idea how I was going to get out of it. Out of any of it.'

He cursed himself. Not so masterful after all.

'Well, then, let's at least get you out of the dress.'

Her brow rose.

'And put on what? A dust sheet? I'm not parading around in front of you in nothing but my underwear.'

'While that is an enticing thought, I was assuming there'd be something in this house for you to wear.'

'Apart from the furniture the house looks pretty empty.'

When he'd inherited this place he'd ordered it cleared of all his grandmother's personal effects. He'd wanted nothing to do with any of them, the memories were too painful. Everything was in storage now. But there might be something they could use, and it would give them something to do and distract her, while he tried her to persuade her to change her mind about the marriage.

He sent her a smile. 'We'll find something for you, Violetta, I promise,' he said, in his most seductive Italian.

He didn't want to look at her in that dress for much longer either. He'd find her something to wear if he had to fashion a dust sheet into something appropriate himself.

Violetta tried to concentrate.

Tried to stop melting every time he spoke in that silky accent. Tried to stop staring at the man and focus on getting to midnight unwed and unseduced.

It was the collarless shirt, or maybe those braces, or just something about the suggestion of being scantly clothed that was so alluring. When had she seen him as anything other than impeccably turned out? This off-duty Leo was thoroughly tempting. Each time he moved the shirt shifted and allowed a glimpse of a broad, muscled breastplate beneath. Why did he have to be such a stunning example of masculine beauty?

'But before I go hunting for a change of clothes, why don't you tell me the real reason you ran away? So far you've revealed you don't like your dress and that no man, including me, has ever paid sufficient attention to you.'

'You make that sound so childish,' she grumbled. 'That's not quite how I meant it. I just want to be seen as an equal, an adult who is perfectly capable of making her sensible decisions.'

'Unfortunately running away from your wedding paints you as immature.'

'Or someone who had no other choice.'

'No choice? All you had to say was, "Leo, I don't want to marry you." See? That easy.'

'You know nothing,' she muttered. 'I would never have been allowed to do that.'

His expression darkened. 'You were being forced into this marriage?'

'No, not exactly.'

'Then what? Why was it so impossible for you to simply say nothing before this point?'

'If I'd told my uncle I didn't want to marry you he would have found some pretence, or argument, to try and persuade me.'

'Point out the many benefits of a match with me, perhaps?' Leo said, sweetly.

Violetta rolled her eyes. 'Probably.'

Leo studied her, eyes narrowed. He shook his head. 'No. I still don't believe you…it feels like you're hiding something.'

Why did he have to be so insistent?

Because he wants the duchy, Violetta. While you're ogling his chest and melting to a puddle every time he speaks Italian, he's probably plotting and planning to get you in front of a priest before nightfall. Does he really care about your objections to the match? No, he believes he knows better and that there are so many advantages to being married to him. Never forget that. He's the enemy, a powerful, self-interested man.

But there was absolutely no way she was telling him the truth. He'd laugh at her, or, worse, insist on marching her back to her uncle. What if the result of that was her uncle just taking power in his own right after all and simply cutting her out of the succession? Maybe he could if she didn't marry and she'd lose everything anyway. Where else could she have run to at the last minute? She'd known the chateau was empty. At one of their joint functions Leo had told her in passing that it was closed up, and she didn't know anywhere else in Grimentz that would be a safe place to hide.

Why did his *grand-mère* have to tell him about those holidays in her cards to him? No one else knew or would have cared. Her mother had never told her uncle where her daughters went for two weeks every summer. He would have considered it beneath his notice and by the time he did notice his niece those holidays had already ceased. So he had no knowledge of Violetta's visits.

She and Luisa had had it all planned. They would hide away in a safe house in the city until midnight. Then go to the cathedral, where she was going to take the flag and swear her allegiance. They were going to film it on their phone and then post it on the Internet for all the world to see. It wasn't much, but it was all she had. She was going to invoke the ancient ritual of swearing allegiance and hope that the people would come with her. But to do that, she had to get back to San Nicolo tonight! Without this man knowing anything of her plans because he'd surely try to stop her. He wanted San Nicolo for himself, as had every Prince of Grimentz for the last four centuries.

She couldn't afford to tell the truth, but she couldn't tell half-truths any more either. He wasn't easily fooled. She'd have to tell a substantial lie and something so profound he'd finally back off.

Violetta turned from him, fixed her attention very deliberately on the dark clouds swirling down from the mountains above, and told perhaps the biggest lie of her young life.

'I'd hoped to spare you this, but the truth is I don't find you at all attractive, quite the opposite in fact.'

At that precise moment, as if the heavens themselves rebelled at that appalling falsehood, a blinding lightning flash illuminated the room, followed by a nerve-jangling thunderclap.

Violetta leapt from her skin. But the man seated behind remained still and silent. There was a long and testing pause until…

'I see.'

That softly spoken response danced across her skin like the brush of warm fingertips.

'In fact…' she said, shivering to hide her real response to him, 'I'm sorry but I couldn't imagine anything less appealing than going to bed with you.'

She couldn't look at him. Those blue eyes would find her out at once.

'Well, then.' He was on his feet behind her.

Was she mistaken or did she just hear a thread of sorrow running through that simple statement? She wondered belatedly if he'd loved Francesca, if her sister's elopement had genuinely wounded him and if she'd hurt him now too.

He came to stand beside her but instead of looking at her he stared up at the skies. Dark roiling clouds chased one another over the valley towards the lake, blocking out the sun and shrouding the gardens and this room in shadows. The man beside her became darker, bigger. Despite the grand dress and priceless tiara, she felt smaller and more insignificant than ever. Because he seemed to have forgotten she was even there. He was studying the lines of trees that ran around the edge of the lawns. They writhed helplessly in the rising wind.

She'd been mistaken. There wasn't a hint of heartbreak in those stern features. He was concerned with something entirely different, and she understood at last.

'It wasn't wolves or basking deer out there before,' she said, gazing up at him. 'It was one of your men, wasn't it?'

Leo exhaled heavily. 'Yes.'

An angry splatter of rain landed on the windows. 'Will they be safe?'

'I ordered them to the gatehouse. They should be there by now.'

Her heart plummeted. How would a car or boat get past Leo's security, now he had them in place? They could only get as far as the gatehouse, but if she could find a way to call Luisa without this man knowing, she could have her send a car to collect her from the gatehouse. They couldn't stop her then.

'Should we think about joining them? If I take off my petticoats I'll fit into the Ferrari.'

'It wouldn't matter if you were in nothing but your underwear,' he said. 'The Ferrari hit a pothole and is out of action.'

'What about the florist's van?' She peered out to the driveway where it sat, lurching back and forth in the wind.

Leo looked at it and back at her. 'No.'

He leant against the counter, his arms folded, head bowed, deep in thought. He wasn't about to demand she tell him the truth, was he? She didn't have another grand lie left in her. She fidgeted, waiting for what he might say next.

'I'm getting hungry,' he announced, and pushed away from the counter.

What?

'I wonder what there is in this kitchen.' He began opening doors, peering in cupboards.

She watched him in disbelief. 'You're worrying about your stomach at a time like this?'

'A man can't think when he's starving.'

'You can't actually be starving. Surely you had breakfast.'

'That was all of…' he glanced at his watch '…six hours ago. If things had gone to plan this morning I should have been fed by now. I burn off a lot of energy, even more so when I'm hungry.'

There was nothing at all in that mundane remark to make her blush. So why were her cheeks turning pink? It was the heat, she decided, and this blasted dress. Maybe she'd calm down if she removed his disquieting presence for a while. Plus, it would give her the chance to try calling Luisa again.

'Why don't you go and look for that change of clothes you promised me, and I'll see if there is anything to eat? Then we can think about how to get to the gatehouse,' she said.

The kitchen door burst open on a violent gust of wind. A flurry of rain, twigs and leaves flew in. Leo leapt to the door and slammed it shut.

'I don't think either of us are going anywhere any time soon,' he said as a crash outside heralded the toppling of plant pots next from the kitchen window.

That declaration that she didn't find him attractive was so obviously a lie. He'd seen the way she looked at him. But he'd respect it. It would just make persuading her to marry him that bit harder.

Right now they had other priorities. The wind had picked up significantly and the florist's van looked in serious danger of turning over. Despite the kitchen being sheltered, at the angle the van was parked, should it start rolling they'd be directly in its path. If they were truly going to be marooned here, they needed this room intact, where there was running water, heat, and hopefully food.

There was no choice. He'd have to move it to safety.

'You can't, it's too dangerous out there.' Violetta placed an anxious hand on his forearm, her small fingers warm against his skin.

'Only for the first ten metres or so. It would be bad for us if we lose the use of this room. I'll move it to the central courtyard. It will be safer there.'

'Then please be careful.' Her brown eyes looked up at him awash with genuine concern. Something warm and needy kicked in his chest. He quashed it. 'I'll be fine. Unlock the courtyard door for me and I'll come back in that way.'

Then he wrenched open the kitchen door, fighting with the wind to pull it shut behind him. Violetta watched him from the kitchen window as he pelted across the gravel and leapt into the driver's seat. As soon as he started moving she also took off, to run through the corridors to the back of the house. Hopefully getting that courtyard door unlocked.

The buffeting of the wind rocked the vehicle back and forth on its chassis. Twigs, leaves, uprooted plants, all were flung at the windscreen as he drove the fifty metres to the U-shaped courtyard that was formed by the wings at the back of the house. As he turned into it the strength of the wind dropped considerably. He could see Violetta wrestling with the key of the door at the end of the courtyard. He parked the van in the most sheltered spot but as he stepped out the heavens opened on another mighty thunderclap. He raced for the door but was soaked through in seconds.

Her anxious face turned up to him, she was shouting but he could barely hear her over the whine of the wind.

'Won't budge...lock stiff...key not turning.'

Leo grasped the handle and tried twisting it from his side. Nothing.

'Stand back,' he yelled and, once she was clear, threw his weight against the door. Still nothing budged. The rain streamed down his face. He could barely see for it. He swept it away with a palm and gave one more almighty yank at the handle.

No movement.

She was frantically searching for another way in, but there was nothing. He was going to have to get back to the kitchen door he'd come out through.

He yelled to Violetta who nodded furiously and took off again. Ready to let him in. He hugged the house as much as he could, but once he'd left the shelter of the courtyard the force of the gale nearly took his feet from under him. He put up a hand to protect his face from all the swirling debris. A branch whipped by and a tangle of twigs wrapped round his ankles, nearly tripping him. He gasped, fighting to breathe as the wind rammed air into his lungs.

His progress back was painfully slow but eventually he reached the kitchen door. Violetta was waiting anxiously at the window and as soon as she saw him, she flew to the door and hauled it open. He staggered in and together they rammed the door shut again. Then both sagged against it, exhausted.

Leo looked down on Violetta. She'd taken a dousing when she opened the door for him. Water dripped down her hair and the front of her dress was drenched. All the perfect silk and lace was stained and smeared with wet leaves. 'That blasted lock. I'm so sorry. It just wouldn't budge.'

'Some wedding day I'm having,' he said and she spluttered, looking up at him with surprised eyes. But her expression changed instantly.

'You're hurt.'

He put his hand up to his forehead. It came back spotted with blood. He frowned at it. 'It's nothing.'

'Sit,' she said, pulling out a chair.

'It's just a cut.'

'Sit,' she ordered and took his arm, pushing him into it. 'There used to be a first aid kit.'

'In the last cupboard by the door.'

He'd sat here before in this kitchen, with cuts or bruises, while Grand-Mère fixed him up, tutting over him and Seb and their fondness for getting into scrapes. One of those rare occasions in his life when he'd known what it was like to have someone care for you who wasn't paid to do so.

Armed with plasters, a towel and antiseptic wipes, she hurried back to him.

She was focused on inspecting the cut above his brow, so he took the opportunity to study her.

Her eyes, he decided, were actually rather fine. Warm and dark. Like the best and bitterest chocolate. They kindled when she was angry with him, or, better still, when she was laughing up at him. He liked how her whole face transformed then.

'You're doing it again.' Violetta had paused in her work.

He raised a brow in question.

'Staring at me.'

'I was just admiring the colour of your eyes,' he said, not looking away. 'I hadn't noticed them before.'

She made a little harrumph in the back of her

throat, but he could tell he'd pleased her. She quickly distracted him in an entirely different way.

He hissed as she dabbed at the cut with a wipe, but she was gentle. Nimble fingers working quickly, cleaning the cut and carefully applying a plaster.

'There, all done.'

'It's not fatal, then?'

'It was a scratch. I thought you were supposed to be some rough tough airborne warrior?' She tutted at him. 'What would your ex-comrades say?' She slanted a saucy look at his parachute badge and the jacket still draped on the chair back. Then set about gathering up the supplies.

'If I'd perished out there it would have saved you a lot of trouble.'

'I'm not going to marry you, so whether you're alive or dead it makes no difference.'

'Your concern for me is heart-warming.'

Interesting that despite her claims to be repelled by the thought of their being intimate together, she'd had no problems touching him.

He'd try an experiment.

As she gathered up the first-aid supplies from the table, he rose to his feet beside her and began unbuttoning his shirt. Her eyes went as big as saucers as he peeled the damp fabric from his shoulders and tugged the sleeves down his arms. Her gaze slewed to his chest and lingered there.

Until she caught his wry expression and went

back to tidying away the supplies. She made three goes as one item after another slipped through her fingers.

'Here.' He picked up the bandage that had rolled for the third time from her grasp. He dropped it on top of the pile she carried.

She turned away. Her ears pink.

The look she'd given him just now was not that of a woman repelled by a man. It was the opposite. He might even say it was hungry for him.

How much did he prefer this blushing, but determined Violetta to the bland, bloodless creature who'd stood meekly by his side at the events they'd attended together?

It felt like the real Violetta, so why had she adopted that fake persona on the other occasions? And what was her real reason for running away from their wedding?

There were still several hours to midnight. The storm might pass in time for them to get back to the castle and wed. *If* he could persuade her to change her mind.

He wasn't giving up on San Nicolo. That was all that mattered here.

CHAPTER FOUR

SHE'D KNOWN HE was a strong, lean god of a man, but that wasn't the same as seeing his muscled chest just inches away...*naked.*

Violetta swallowed and cursed her flaming face. She buried her head in the cupboard and took longer than necessary to put away the medical supplies.

His skin was tanned to a deep gold, as if he spent a good deal of time outdoors with his shirt off. When did he find the time?

The lines of muscle she glimpsed were deeply fascinating. She wanted to run her fingers along them, or her lips. She made a strange little sound of shock and stood up abruptly.

He was shrugging back into his jacket, and she couldn't decide which emotion had the upper hand.

Relief or disappointment.

He didn't button the jacket up so as he moved there were more glimpses of that muscled breast-plate. The silky skin and the line of dark hair running down his abdomen and disappearing into his waistband.

'We can't stay in these wet things.' Violetta was patting at her hair with a towel. 'I'm bad enough but you're absolutely soaked through. We need dry clothes.'

Costumes? Of course.

'I wonder if Grand-Mère's costume gallery is still there,' Leo mused.

Violetta brightened. 'From her parties? Will it still be there?'

'I ordered all her personal effects be placed in storage when she died. But the costumes may have been left with the other fixtures and fittings.'

Throughout their marriage his maternal grandparents had held a masked ball every year, one of the most sought-after invites on the European social calendar. Grand-Mère had continued the tradition even after her husband's death and after every ball she'd kept a selection of the costumes worn. Her own and her husband's, and many donated by guests.

'I'll go and see if it's still here and you can check the pantries for food.'

Leo headed for the grand staircase. Time alone to think.

All those things she'd said of him earlier. How he'd behaved towards her when they'd met at official functions. Had he really become that man? As cold and unfeeling as his father? It shocked him.

The empty house echoed to the sound of his footsteps as he crossed the marble tiles of the hallway. Chateau Elisabetha had never felt so forlorn, because his grandmother had always been there. Seb too and a handful of servants. It bothered him that the place felt so lonely now. It didn't seem right somehow. After it had always felt so alive with his *grand-mère* in residence.

Most of her things had gone, but the staff who'd cleared the house had missed the odd item, such as the CD player in the kitchen.

On the landing were several portraits that over the years Grand-Mère had commissioned of her beloved dogs. They watched him as he passed, shaming him with their patient, unconditional devotion. One-eyed, one-eared, balanced on three legs, whatever their imperfection, each had been painted to make the viewer see them as perfect and as well beloved as they'd been to their owner.

Leo went by, ignoring the reproachful eyes.

He passed the family and guest bedrooms and up the stairs to the final floor.

Under the eaves of this wing ran an attic. Its entire length had been fitted with wardrobes. Leo opened the first.

Bingo.

Carefully wrapped in linen covers sat line after line of his grandmother's beloved costumes. He checked out the first. An extravagant blue dress with hopped petticoats and an elaborate white wig: Marie Antoinette had once graced the ball. The next, in sharp contrast, was a cheerleader outfit, in burgundy and gold with Grimentz High emblazoned across the front and complete with a set of matching pom-poms.

Unbidden came lustful thoughts of Violetta, ministering to some of his baser needs while dressed in it. Well, well, looked as if his prim runaway was stirring his blood after all.

'What are you grinning about?'

He looked up to find Violetta in the doorway.

'I was imagining you in this,' he said, holding up the short dress and giving the pom-poms a cheery shake.

'Well, I'm about to wipe that smile from your face. I've searched the kitchen and the larder. Apart from tinned stuff there isn't a single fresh, edible thing in this house.'

Leo allowed his gaze to wander in a slow appraisal from the tips of her toes, past that slender waist, the subtle swell of her breasts and her small, currently belligerent mouth. Eventually he met her eye.

'Oh, I wouldn't say that.'

She rolled her eyes, pretending outrage but he noted the flush of red across her cheeks.

She marched over to the closet where the female outfits were stored and riffled through them. Opening the first to check the contents, finding the elaborate wig and blue gown.

'Marie Antoinette? Not a chance, I'm not enjoying the similarities.'

More bags were unzipped. A mermaid. A gladiatrix. A ballerina ready for the starring role in *Swan Lake*. On that one she paused. Stroking the snowy white feathers adorning the tutu.

Leo watched as she gave a little sigh and moved on. Suddenly, he hoped she'd already discounted the cheerleader outfit, thinking it might be better for him if she didn't choose it.

But back she came.

'As you were so taken with the idea of me in this, perhaps I'll wear it,' she said, taking it from his hands with a challenge in her eyes that sent a sharp kick of lust straight to his groin.

There was the rapid clatter of heels on the stairs, then the opening and closing of a door as she entered one of the bedrooms on the floor below.

Leo blew out a long breath. Feeling unaccountably…*rattled.*

The gale outside buffeted the rafters and a draught chilled his skin through his damp shirt. He needed to find something dry to wear.

He crossed the attic to the other set of cupboards where he thought to find all the male costumes his grandmother had saved.

But the first wasn't male at all, and, sadly for him, the woman who'd worn it was well known to him. It had belonged to his mother.

Prince Friedrich had been strict about what costumes his wife had been allowed to wear. He'd had final approval on her choice and it had always had to be something exalted and dignified. A heroine from mythology or a celebrated monarch or leader. No mermaids or gladiators were allowed for Giovanna von Frohburg.

Leo drew the lapis-blue headdress of Queen Nefertiti from its protective covering. He vividly remembered the year she'd worn it.

He'd been accustomed to seeing his mother dressed for grand occasions, but this costume had so suited her fine-boned beauty that from his hiding place on the landing outside his rooms he'd been transfixed watching her descend the stairs on her husband's arm.

His beautiful mother, whom he'd adored.

And who'd abandoned him.

Prince Friedrich had had his choice from the cream of European aristocracy from which to take a wife. He'd chosen badly.

Giovanna had loved her status but not the expectations and restrictions that went with it. Nor had she loved the man who'd elevated her to her lofty position by making her his wife. He had been too serious and strict, too obsessed with regaining the grand duchy. And too averse to anything that might constitute fun. No one had been surprised when his beautiful young wife had sought her entertainment and then male affection elsewhere. The only real surprise was how long she'd actually stayed with her husband. When she'd finally departed Leo was a teenager.

At fourteen, with all the swagger of youth, he'd imagined himself a man. But not on the day his mother had left. That day he'd wept like the child he still was.

Seb had burst into his room.

'You'd better come. Your parents have had an enormous row and now Aunt Giovanna is leaving.'

Leo had found her rooms in uproar. Servants hurriedly packing clothes into trunks. Footmen hefting them to the hallways. His mother sweeping make-up and pots of lotions into a vanity case.

'Don't go,' he'd begged her.

'I've found a wonderful man to love me,' she'd answered, snapping the case closed. 'Not like your father.'

'But I love you,' Leo had cried.

She'd patted his cheek absently. 'I know, darling. I'll see you soon. I promise.'

He'd followed her to the castle forecourt, all the while pleading with her not to leave him. When that had no effect, he'd flung himself at her. There had followed an unseemly tussle, where his mother's security team had been forced to physically prise his arms from about her neck.

As her car had borne her away his cousin had tried to comfort him, but Seb had been younger, smaller and Leo, wild with grief, had been having none of it. He'd shoved him away.

Servants had averted their eyes. Tight-jawed castle guards had stared straight ahead. Seb, on his backside on the cobbles where Leo had pushed him, had sobbed openly.

At a first-floor window a lone, impassive figure had stared down on the scene. The only one to witness his teenage son's humiliation and remain unmoved.

All Leo's pain and rage had coalesced on him. He'd stormed up the stairs and barged into his father's study.

'You did this,' he'd yelled. 'You drove her away.'

His father had advanced towards him, arms outstretched, and Leo remembered feeling stunned that his father might be about to change a habit of a lifetime and embrace his only child.

How wrong he had been. With one hand he had grasped Leo's shoulder, with the other he had slapped him hard across the cheek.

'Stop making a spectacle and control yourself, boy. You're a prince, not a commoner.'

Leo had folded inwards. His own hand against his stinging cheek. Shocked by the sudden eruption of violence that had disappeared as quickly. His father had been in command of himself.

'I gave your mother a choice. She could have her lover, but she'd never be permitted to see you again. She chose him.'

The anguish of that simple truth had sliced through Leo's heart. The mother he adored had abandoned him to a father she knew was heartless and cold. It had been the defining moment of his life as he'd vowed there and then never to let anyone close again.

He'd stood and showed no emotion while his father had poured a storm of recrimination over his head.

'She left because of you. You were too demanding, too clingy. What kind of monarch will you be if you can't control yourself? You shame the great name of von Frohburg.'

As something had broken for good inside him, Leo had stared at a blank strip of wall between two portraits of his most illustrious and pompous-looking forebears. He'd hated those portraits ever after and they were the first things he had consigned to some backwater of the palace the moment that study had become his.

Leo had never again tried to do anything to please his father. Quite the opposite. He'd embraced disobedience, courted disrepute. He would have been expelled from school but for the cachet his title had brought to the place. As the years had passed, and Leo had matured into a man, observers had been hard pressed to say who had cut the most scandalous swathe through the opposite sex. He or his mother. She was on husband number four. Leo had scores of conquests, most of whom

he barely remembered. For a while he had been
the undisputed wild child of Europe. Even Sebastien, with his title, good looks and easy charm,
had been in second place. The aloof heir to the
Grimentzian throne had been too much of a draw.

But Leo had never forgotten the scorn and the
blame of his father's verbal thrashing. Since that
day he'd never allowed a moment's true emotion
to be on display. Perhaps that was why Francesca
had eloped. Had he become too like his father?

Exploring that now wouldn't help. He had the
other girl to persuade to the altar instead.

Leo held the Nefertiti crown up to the light.
His grandmother had kept her daughter's most
celebrated costume.

Giovanna's departure had hurt Grand-Mère too.
She'd become a pariah overnight. She had been
denied all access to her only grandchild. He'd believed it when it was revealed she'd helped her
daughter by allowing the lovers to meet in secret
in Chateau Elisabetha. Leo had felt so betrayed
he'd never forgiven her, even as an adult, when
she'd written to him, explaining herself. She knew
her daughter was selfish and spoiled but she loved
her and wanted her to be happy, and she hoped
maybe one day he would understand sacrificing
something for love.

Never. He would never understand that. Love
was such a fleeting unreliable emotion to hitch

anything to. He'd never made the mistake of loving anything again.

Every summer an invite had arrived for him to
visit her. He'd never even replied. She'd spent the
rest of her year in France, close to the capital. All
those times he'd been in Paris, he'd never once
gone to see her, and she would have known he'd
been there. He and Seb always made the headlines—for all the wrong reasons.

Still, a handwritten card and carefully chosen
gift had arrived every birthday and Christmas,
and when she'd died she'd left him this house.

With the bequest had come a brief message.

*You were happy here once. Perhaps you
could be again, if you try, my darling boy.*

The old woman hadn't deserved his treatment
of her. She'd loved her daughter. Selfish, shallow,
dazzling Giovanna.

But how did you punish a mother who didn't
care if you lived or died? You punished her kin.

'I'm going to need your help getting out of my
dress.'

Framed in the doorway stood another woman
determined to get what she wanted no matter the
cost to him.

His mother. Francesca. Now Violetta.

He shoved the Nefertiti headdress back with
the rest of the costume and closed the door on it.

'I thought we'd established you'd find my touch repellent?' he drawled.

'I'm only asking you to cut me out of my dress. I think I can cope with that.'

'Cut you out? You're sewn into it? Women still do that?' he asked, surprised.

'Women like me still have that done to them, I think you mean. What woman in her right mind wants to be stuck in something she can't get out of without help? Why do you think I ran away in it?'

She turned on her heel.

Leo sighed and set off after her. He was going to be damp for a little longer.

Violetta felt those cool blue eyes burning a hole in her back as he followed her down the stairs to the room she had chosen to change in.

What had possessed her to challenge him in that way before? She'd chosen that cheerleader dress because she'd liked something in his expression, flirting? She was supposed to be repelled by him.

Now they struck another problem.

'I thought it would just tear once I tugged at it. I didn't even try back at the castle—there was no time. But I can't even get the two tiny buttons on the neck undone, never mind the rest of it.' She reached up to fiddle with the tiny silk-covered buttons. 'See, nothing budges.'

She peered over her shoulder at him. 'Have you anything to cut it with?'

'On me? No, of course not.'

'Don't you have a Swiss army knife or something? I thought the Grimentzian Guard were famously prepared for anything.'

'Normally, I never leave the castle without one,' he said, tartly. 'But curiously, I hadn't imagined I'd need it on my wedding day.'

'I've looked through the drawers and in the en-suite bathroom, but all personal effects have indeed been removed from the rooms, just as you'd said. There isn't so much as a pair of nail scissors to be had.'

Her teeth chattered.

'I can go hunting for a knife but you're shivering in that wet dress. You need to get out of it quickly. I'll try tearing it.'

His fingers landed on the back of her dress. Exploring what she assumed was a neatly sewn seam. He gave an exploratory tug, but nothing budged. He tugged again, harder. It rocked her on her feet.

His fingers brushed the nape of her neck. Violetta swallowed hard. Heat poured through her.

'Forgive me. I'm going to have to touch you.'

Wasn't that what he'd already been—?

Oh...

When he said touch, she didn't know he meant with his mouth.

Warm lips brushed the back of her neck. Then bared teeth as he used them to tear at the threads. The faintest scrape of stubble as his jaw moved against her skin. Violetta clutched the cheerleader dress harder, willing the torture to end, or wanting it never to stop. She wasn't sure which. Every nerve ending at the back of her neck was on fire.

Then, mercifully, a ripping sound and cool air hitting her spine. He ripped some more, until the dress flapped open to the base of her spine.

'Will that do?' He sounded hoarse.

She wriggled out of the lace sleeves and bodice. But she wore so many petticoats there was no way she could simply step out of the dress. She needed to lift it over her head, and she was going to need his help.

She peeked back at him. He was staring at her spine.

'Um, I need your help to get this off.'

His gaze lifted back to her face.

'Yes, of course.' He was behind her. Grabbing the skirt of the dress to lift it upwards. It caught in the tiara, and it took a moment of struggling to release it again.

Her hands went across her breasts. She heard the moment Leo saw his next challenge. An odd, strangled sound in his throat. The petticoats were fixed with a drawstring and bow at the back. It needed loosening.

His fingers were at her back again. She felt a

little tug and the petticoat fell with a whoosh to puddle at her feet.

'I'm not looking,' he said, sounding even more strangled.

She quickly shimmied into the sleeveless mini-dress and glanced over her shoulder. Her former groom hadn't lied, he didn't so much as peek. Instead, he was wrestling manfully with her gown, trying to lay it carefully over the bed, looking a little hot and bothered. Not his usual composed self.

She reached around for the zip, discovering she had a new difficulty.

'I need you to fasten this one up.'

Would this torture ever end?

Leo had peeked. He'd pretended not to, of course, but he saw the shapely bottom, the limber thighs, the frou-frou of bridal underwear. He masked his reaction by focusing all his attention on dealing with the mountain of a dress. Hell, how had the woman managed to run even a metre in it? Despite the inconvenience she'd caused by fleeing, he had a new grudging respect for her.

Yards of silk. Acres of petticoats. Had this genuinely been their wedding night all his ardour might have been dampened by the sheer bloody effort of getting her out of it.

Until he saw what was beneath. Tearing all those neat, tiny stitches keeping her in had given him ample opportunity to study the delicate bone structure of her spine and the perfection of her skin.

What was wrong with him? She wasn't his type, nothing like it, but his heart still racketed about in his chest as he drew closer.

Because every inch of her spine was on show, and he itched to place his fingers back on her exposed skin and not cover it all up.

Perhaps it was because she'd said he repelled her.

He knew that was a lie. He wasn't blind, he could see how he affected her. But whatever her reason for not being truthful, he would respect her choice and not touch her unless absolutely necessary.

He stood behind her, grasped the zip in the cheerleader outfit and tugged it closed, then stepped back.

'How does it look?' she asked, turning to face him.

Too short. Showing too much leg. Too cute…

He shoved his hands in his pockets. 'Fine. Except for…' He nodded towards her head.

'What?' She froze. 'It's not a spider, is it?'

'No. It's an irreplaceable tiara.'

'Oh.' Her hand shot to her hair. 'I completely forgot. Poor Elisabetha. I doubt she'd ever thought it would be used like this. Could this be the most expensive cheerleader outfit in history?' She giggled.

It was a simple female laugh.

Nothing to get all bothered about.

So why had the effect of it shot straight to his groin?

He cleared his throat. 'I'm going to see what else there is up here that we could use, in case the weather gets worse.'

The house phone ringing in the hallway halted him. Violetta hovered close by as Leo answered.

'Okay, we'll sit tight here, then.'

He replaced the receiver.

'What is it? What's happened?'

'Sadly, you will be stuck with me for a while. That was my head of security. The road between here and the gatehouse is blocked by a fallen tree.'

'Don't they have four by fours? Can't they just drive round it?'

'If they could don't you think they'd have said that?'

She flew to the window. 'But I have to get back to San Nicolo tonight.'

'Perhaps you should have fled there, then,' he said. When she looked stricken, he added more gently, 'Look, this weather is already much worse than predicted so who knows? But it will be to-morrow now at the earliest.'

'Tomorrow? I have to be back in San Nicolo before then. My uncle might...oh, never mind.'

'Trust me, I've no more desire to be trapped

alone here together than you. But we've no choice, so we need to make the best of it.'

'I wouldn't be in this mess at all if it weren't for you,' she railed at him. 'You planned all of this. I just know it,' she muttered.

'Yes, that's me.' He flourished a hand through the air. 'At my command tempests blow and storms rage.'

'Why don't you use your powers to make me disappear and then you can have the grand duchy without the need to marry anyone at all?'

'Why don't you stop behaving like a spoiled child and do something useful, like help me search the house for things we might need now we're stuck here for the night?'

A spoiled child?

Who'd ever spoilt her? Who in her family had treated her as if she mattered at all?

No one.

Ever.

That blistering injustice sent her rage soaring.

'It's your damn house. You can do it yourself,' she shouted and slammed the bedroom door in his face.

CHAPTER FIVE

VIOLETTA PACED THE ROOM. What was she going to do now? How was she going to get back to the duchy in time to claim the throne?

The simple answer was she couldn't, and she feared her uncle might snatch it out from beneath her by claiming it for himself. Would he dare do that? Legally he wouldn't have that right but, since she'd run away, could he portray her as being unfit to rule and persuade the duchy's ministers to back him as Grand Duke?

None of her careful planning with Luisa had imagined this scenario. Being trapped in Grimentz and with the one man she'd hoped to get away from.

Footsteps sounded overhead. Her tormentor was back in the attics.

She scowled up at the ceiling. If she were really lucky, he might encounter a few rotten floorboards to fall through and be stuck up there, out of her way, until this was all over.

When he was near, she found it too hard to focus.

She rubbed the back of her neck, remembering those perfect white teeth nibbling at the nape of her neck, the searing heat of his lips. She'd felt the effect everywhere.

She shook herself. There was no time for thinking of that. She had to work out what to do next.

Could she risk trying to phone Luisa again while he was prowling about upstairs? What if he heard her and came down demanding to know who she was talking to? Would his team at the gatehouse be able to intercept her call? Her mobile had been taken away from her last night. At least, it wasn't in her rooms when her possessions had been unpacked. They'd told her it was with her other luggage. She'd asked for it, but no one had brought it to her.

There went those footsteps overhead again. She scowled up at the ceiling. This was his doing, she was certain. He'd deliberately isolated her in his chateau.

He was coming back downstairs now. Violetta stopped pacing; it wasn't helping. What could she do? No one was getting anywhere near the chateau until the storm had passed anyway.

She regretted that silly remark about him causing the storm. It made her sound like the witless female her uncle thought she was.

She didn't entirely trust Leo, but she'd jilted

him, not the other way round. A second Della Torre sister to humiliate him in the most public of ways and, so far, he'd been rather forgiving and decent to her.

But beneath all that he was still the enemy. A powerful man who'd in the end expect her to do as he wanted.

She stepped out of her high-heeled wedding shoes. She was wearing a different costume now and she'd be a different Violetta to match. Plus, she knew where there was footwear that suited her much more.

She left her tiara where it was. She liked how it flashed and glittered in the low light. It reminded her that she was not only a princess but about to be a grand duchess too. She wouldn't let any man stop her, however powerful—or divinely attractive—he was.

Elisabetha's tiara was staying put.

They both had a job to do. And no matter how fast he made her heart beat, Leo von Frohburg had no part in it.

In a foul temper, Leo stalked off down the landing.

How dared she blame him for their predicament when it was she who'd chosen to flee to this God-forsaken valley and its cursed chateau with all the conflicting memories it held for him?

He reached the attic stairs and took them three

at a time. Pretending it was solely anger that drove him upwards, and nothing to do with the temptation of a delicate spine, of warm skin the colour of honey and a telling shudder of desire when he placed his mouth to a sensitive neck.

Whatever her real reason for fleeing their wedding was, it certainly wasn't due to a lack of attraction.

In the line of wardrobes, Leo found some dry clothes and quickly changed.

As he dressed, he considered how to deal with Violetta. His belief that he'd easily persuade her to marry had quickly foundered on his bride's hostility. He was going to have to dig deeper if he was ever to win her over.

Leo wasn't accustomed to dealing with females beyond a date or two—he always ended things before they got messy and never stayed to deal with the fallout. He was a charming dinner companion and a generous lover but that was the extent of his interactions. He simply didn't do protracted relationships with women. He'd learned the impact of that the hard way.

In fact, he barely did personal relationships at all. Only Seb was allowed close and even he was often kept at arm's length.

His easy path to the grand duchy had been blocked by the weather, but it was still in his sights.

For now, they were trapped here and there was

nothing he could do about it, so he focused instead on what he could control. He made a mental tally of precisely where they stood.

They had shelter and basic foodstuffs. They had extra clothing, of sorts.

While he was obliged to keep his hands off her, that cheerleader outfit was proving to be too distracting for comfort.

He wandered the house, checking the guest suites and family bedrooms first, looking for anything they could use for an overnight stay, but beneath the dust sheets they'd all been stripped of their linens.

In the servants' quarters he had more luck, finding two small rooms with a made-up single bed and en-suite bathroom each. He found a supply of unopened toiletries, including toothbrushes and shampoos.

The rooms also faced away from the worst of the weather. At least they might be able to sleep despite the gale blowing outside. The storm was getting worse, and the old house creaked and groaned as the wind tore round it.

On the ground floor the storerooms yielded up torches and storm lanterns. A pantry held a stash of candles and matches. Yet there was no radio and no TV in any of the rooms. If they were to have any entertainment tonight it would be coming from his *grand-mère*'s battered CD-player or themselves.

Under other circumstances there would be some pleasant ways for them to while away a few hours together.

He thought again of Violetta's slender spine. The perfect legs and buttocks in those sheer panties.

Perhaps they didn't have to sleep separately. Perhaps he could persuade her to join him in his bed. Perhaps they could return to the palace tomorrow and actually wed.

Once he'd discovered the real reason she ran away.

There wasn't another man in the equation, he was certain of that. She would have said so. It would have been the easiest way to extricate herself from the wedding. Instead, she'd chosen to make up some lie about finding him repellent.

Leo gathered up his supplies and headed back to the kitchens.

Why was it so imperative that she get back to San Nicolo tonight?

Unless…

Could she be honestly thinking of trying to take power in her own right? A woman who'd been carefully trained only to be the perfect wife to the monarch, not the monarch herself.

Her uncle had said she had no aptitude for the work, but perhaps she'd concealed her true identity from him as well.

She wasn't in the kitchen when he returned with

his finds. He dumped everything on the table and went off searching for her.

He called to her, but the servants' quarters remained silent.

The door back to the hallway stood open and beyond that he heard sounds coming from the ballroom.

In the hall the door to the ballroom stood ajar. The shutters in there were closed and the room was filled with shadows. Then Leo saw a flicker of movement.

Violetta was there, in the centre of the room.

His gaze slid inexorably down those slender legs. She'd returned to the costume cupboards in the attics and filched the ballet shoes. Their ribbon ties criss-crossed her ankles. As he watched she rose up en pointe and sketched out a few steps.

Ballet.

There'd always been a certain gracefulness to how she moved, a pleasing fluidity. Now he understood why.

She wove unhurried, elegant moves through the half-light. A series of pirouettes, an arabesque, a leap, as graceful as a gazelle, where she appeared to almost hover in mid-air.

Unnoticed Leo watched, transfixed by the heart-stopping grace on show as Violetta danced. Lucky would be the man who held the heart of a girl who had the passion to dance like that.

In the dim hallway Leo scowled at nothing in particular. When had he become so fanciful?

She saw him and stopped abruptly, mid-move. She marched towards the doorway to exit the room and shut the door firmly behind her, as if she could expunge the memory of what he'd seen.

Certain it was seared on his memory for ever, Leo ached to see more.

'I'm sorry,' she said. 'I suppose I should have been looking for useful things, but it's just—'

'That you dance,' he said, almost in wonder.

She shot him a wary glance. 'Something like that.'

'And that open space called to you?' Leo tipped his chin in the direction of the ballroom.

'Well, yes.' Her expression was guarded but her eyes glittered through the gloom.

'I'm the same when the wind is fair and the lake calls to me. I just want to be out there sailing.' He smiled down on her. 'It feels like flying.'

She studied him, and he could tell he'd surprised her. She apparently knew as little about him as he knew of her.

With a swift move she slipped round him to start off across the hallway. 'Let's hope you're better at that than you are flying for real,' she said, perhaps trying to deflect the attention from her. He ignored her teasing.

'It was very beautiful,' he said to her back.

She flung a glance over her shoulder. The tiara

glinted at him, the gaudy cheerleader dress with its pleated skirt revealing so much leg. She was a tiny punk ballerina and he wanted to watch her move again.

'Will you dance for me later?'

'Absolutely not. Apart from my tutors, I don't dance for anyone else.'

That struck him as tragic because he'd glimpsed something that was beyond simple beauty.

She'd disappeared back through the service entrance.

On a sigh Leo set off after her. This woman was drawing more from him than he'd ever expected.

Violetta's heart raced. No one had ever seen her dance. No one.

When Leo arrived in the kitchen, he looked at her as if she were a conundrum he'd just solved, and with a warmth in his gaze that sent an answering heat coiling in her belly.

'So why do you never dance for an audience?' he asked, continuing a conversation she'd hoped they'd ended. 'You're a gifted dancer.'

'It's not about that. It's…'

He'd thrown the light switch in the kitchen and now they were out of the shadows she could see what he was wearing.

She stared at him. 'Out of everything up there, that's what you chose?'

His choice of 'costume' was a white collarless shirt and formal black trousers. Identical to what he'd been wearing before they were both drenched.

'So I'm dressed as a cheerleader with a ballet addiction and you're dressed as what? Yourself?'

'It's appropriate,' he said.

'There's no one else here to see you but me. Can't you let your hair down a little?'

He looked as if she'd suggested he prance naked along his castle battlements. Violetta shook her head at him. 'It's all true, isn't it? You really don't have a fun side.'

'There isn't much time for fun when you're the leader of a country.'

'You're not a leader here. We're just two people stuck in this house together. Surely you could relax a bit.'

'In the same way that you could let me see you dance?' he said.

She scowled at him. 'It's not the same at all.'

His gaze grew warm, his expression softened. *'Allora, dimmi perché?'* he asked. Then tell me why. Said too gently and in Italian.

She wished he wouldn't do that. Again it whispered over her skin. Why couldn't he stay the uninterested creature he'd been before?

'It's just for me. It's always been just for me.'

'So you've said but that still doesn't explain why. Please, I'd like to know.'

She shuffled a foot en pointe back and forth,

wondering how much to share. Wondering how it was he made her *want* to share.

'It's because it feels like a rebellion against all the strictures placed on my life.'

'Go on.'

Outside a poplar tree swayed back and forth in the gale. Despite the forces at work, it still looked graceful and strong.

'When my sister ran away and I became heir to the duchy, any small freedoms I'd been allowed were instantly curtailed. My father had always been strict, but it became even worse after Francesca left. He took everything but ballet. That he allowed me to keep. He said it would keep me slender and give me poise, so I'd look good for you and be a credit to you. As if that was all I could ever be. An addendum to you.'

His brow knotted. 'I'm sorry. That's not what I would have wanted.'

'Isn't it?' She speared him with an angry glare. 'Isn't that precisely what you wanted from me? You'd have taken the time to get to know me better otherwise.'

His mouth opened but he closed it again. He remained silent. She was right.

'Despite that, they didn't drive the joy of dance out of me. I love it,' she said. 'The creativity. The hidden strength behind the beautiful, sinuous shapes I can make with my body. But I won't share that. My family never cared about what I could achieve.'

And neither would Leo, she thought, despite his apparent interest now. He just wanted to persuade her to marry him.

'That's why, apart from my dancing tutors and a few classmates, no one has ever seen me perform.'

When required she danced with partners at social occasions with the staid gliding around the floor, but, while she was graceful, she'd never once set free her dancing heart.

She'd learned long ago to conceal her true self. It was so easy to be dismissed and ridiculed. She remembered her mother, forever deferring to her husband, undermined and excluded. Gradually losing all faith that she could make a decision herself. Becoming precisely the kind of creature her menfolk imagined she was all along. Francesca had eloped to save herself, but that was not going to be Violetta's fate. She would have her independence. She'd learned to bide her time. She would achieve her dreams and she'd have them on her terms.

Leo was the only thing standing in the way of that. However charming he was being right now.

She must remember he'd had her staff removed. It must have been him because why would her uncle have done that? The regent had little interest in her, yes, but cruel? No. She doubted he actually gave his niece a moment's thought once she'd left her weekly, perfunctory meetings with him. He was too busy running the duchy, so why would he have arranged for her staff to be dismissed?

It all pointed to her future husband, making sure his bride was only surrounded by those loyal to him, so he could do exactly what he wanted in the grand duchy.

Well, he wasn't getting his hands on it.

Even if those hands were beautiful. Her neck tingled at the memory of his fingers moving across her skin.

She moved away from him, putting the kitchen table between them. He narrowed his eyes on her, sensing the shift in her mood perhaps.

'Now you're being so frank, why don't you tell me the real reason you won't marry me?' It was quietly spoken but a steely certainty ran through it. It said, I know you're lying. 'When I touched you before your shudder had nothing to do with revulsion. As you so charmingly mentioned earlier, I've had enough experience to know the difference.'

He came round the table towards her, removing the only barrier between them. He was lean and powerful. A prowling wolf on the hunt and she had nowhere to run. She gripped a chair back so hard her knuckles turned white.

What could he do if she told him now? Nothing. They were trapped here until tomorrow at least. Her instinct was to get this over with, be honest with him. After what she'd done today, perhaps she owed him that after all. She released her grip on the chair, turned and lifted her chin to stare right into those fierce eyes.

Facing him down.

'All right, I'll tell you. I won't marry you because I plan to be Grand Duchess in my own right. As soon as I get home, I'll claim the throne as the rightful heir. Then I'm going to give San Nicolo its freedom and make it a democracy.'

As if all the dark fates in the world had aligned for a second time that day the room was filled by the dazzling white light of a lightning flash.

Leo's face was stark with shock in the split second of eerie light.

Then another mighty, foundation-rattling thunderclap crashed directly overhead.

The power went out and Violetta shrieked.

In the gloom she saw Leo's shadowy figure head to the phone. He picked it up then slammed it back into the cradle with a curse.

'The line's gone dead.'

He grabbed a torch from the stash on the table. 'I'll check the fuse box.'

When he came back the kitchen light remained off.

'The power is out too.'

'What do we do now?' She looked about her helplessly.

'Same as before. We wait it out. We have candles and a gas cooker. We'll manage.'

Violetta wrapped her arms about her, suddenly feeling chilled. Not just trapped with this man, but now in the dark too.

'Okay.' She pulled herself together. 'We have to make the best of it. I'll find something to eat.'

She rummaged around in the pantry, found two tins.

She held them aloft. 'Coq au vin or beef bourguignon?'

'*Canned* coq au vin?' Leo said, eyeing both with distaste.

'Or we could push the boat out and have baked lentils and sausage.'

Leo grimaced. 'What a shame you hadn't fled in a catering van. We might have had something better to eat.'

'You can talk.' Violetta grabbed a can opener and a saucepan. 'You drove our only other transport straight into a ditch.'

'I did not drive into a ditch. It was an unavoidable pothole, which I would have never encountered had I not been out searching for you.'

'And yet I managed to avoid it.' She opened the tin and tipped the contents into the pan.

'You were not driving a million euros' worth of Ferrari.'

'No, the florist's van is much more practical and useful.' She sat the pan on the stove.

'Ah, yes,' he said. 'Just what one needs when stranded miles from civilisation with no power and little food, floral arrangements.'

He came closer and bent to take a tentative sniff at the contents of the saucepan. When he looked up at her his expression was pained.

'That's the beef bourguignon,' Violetta explained.

'It smells utterly delightful. One can only imagine the taste.'

'At least we have something to eat. What about your men at the gatehouse? Aren't they just as stranded as we are?'

Leo stared out at the pelting rain and the trees writhing in the wind.

'They should count themselves fortunate if they've been spared the horrors of canned beef bourguignon. Though I suspect the gatehouse will be similarly stocked.'

Then his face brightened. 'But they won't have a wine cellar. With any luck there might be a bottle or two still there.' He disappeared with the torch again and when he returned a few minutes later he clutched two bottles of wine.

'These might mask the taste of what you are about to serve from that pan.' He dug a bottle opener out of a drawer. 'It may be the only way I can bring myself to eat it.'

'I thought you were starving?'

'Sadly I haven't lost my taste buds.'

She busied herself finding cutlery, bowls and two glasses for the wine.

'You seem very at home in this kitchen,' Leo said.

'Your *grand-mère* loved to cook. We spent a lot of time together here.'

'It was the same when Seb and I came to stay. She'd set us to work. Shelling peas, chopping herbs. We did it because we knew the food would be good. She was an excellent cook,' he said with a doleful look at the empty can by the stove.

'She taught me, too. I'd often cook for Luisa and sometimes Rolfe.'

When he looked blank, she added, 'My dresser and my personal secretary. At least they were until you had them removed.'

His gaze turned icy. 'You think I did that? To what purpose? If they were removed without your consent, it was your uncle's doing!'

She didn't want to believe that. Her uncle wasn't affectionate—much like her father, he saw her only as a commodity to serve the duchy—but he'd not been deliberately cruel.

'Why would he do that?' She couldn't keep the hurt from her voice.

His expression softened. 'I'm sorry, but my guess would be to isolate you by removing your support network. Do you think he had any inkling you weren't going to go through with the marriage?'

She shook her head. 'I was so careful to appear willing.'

'You certainly fooled me.'

She sent him a glance from beneath her lashes. 'I had to. I'd planned to disappear the night before the wedding and hide in a safe house in the city. But then my uncle said that the arrangements had changed. I was going to spend my last night in Grimentz not San Nicolo. I thought that was your doing too.'

He raised a brow.

'Okay, I get it, that wasn't you either.'

She spooned the contents of the pan into bowls and put them down in the two places she'd set at the table. Leo filled their glasses and then sat.

He took a tentative spoonful of the beef dish.

Violetta watched the muscles of his jaw as he chewed. Such a mundane act shouldn't be so fascinating. He swallowed, took a quick swig of wine.

'And?' she asked.

'Not the worst dish I've ever tasted, but the bar is pretty low. In the survival course of my army training, a sergeant once served up a worm omelette.'

She laughed and started on her own bowl of food.

'So why do you want to give San Nicolo its democracy so badly?' he asked.

'Because I've lived a life with so little chance to determine my fate. I understand the position my people are in. I've seen first-hand how their chances have been limited by the offices of the grand duke and now the regent. Unlike my family the people have shown me nothing but love and I want to give back to them.'

Leo nodded. 'You saw something first-hand? Something in particular?'

'I think it all began with one person. Being dismissed yourself is one thing, but seeing it happen to a boy who didn't have the compensation of the privileged life I had sowed a seed in me. From then it just grew and grew.'

'What boy? Was he a sweetheart of yours?'

An odd gruffness to his voice made her look up. Those blue eyes were unreadable in the low light, but his expression was curiously intense.

'No, nothing like that. I actually only met him on one occasion but the memory of it has stayed with me for years.

'I was only eleven, I'd accompanied my parents on an official visit to a food festival. We're big on those in San Nicolo. Food and wine make up our biggest exports. A teenage boy had entered his farm's cheese in one of the competitions and he should have won. It was the best there that day, but my parents gave the prize to one of their cronies. I tried to argue with my mother about it, but she told me, in no uncertain terms, to be quiet and remember my place.' She shrugged. 'I know it probably sounds insignificant to you.'

'Not at all. It's those small moments that shape who we are.'

'I don't know why I even tried to make a difference. My parents never listened to me. I was a second daughter when what they wanted was a son. My mother used to look at me as if it were my fault. She tried to raise us in the way she thought appropriate to our futures but there was no love in it.'

'Did you love her?' Leo asked.

'Who doesn't try to love their parents? Until it becomes obvious you're a big fat disappointment to them. Is it terrible to say that I didn't miss them much after they were gone? Uncle Guido at least showed some minor interest in me, even if it was only to get me ready to be a wife to you.'

'And we know how successful he was doing that!' Leo said. But this time she couldn't feel any humour in it.

'My parents poured all their efforts into getting Francesca ready to be your grand duchess, but in the end she hadn't even wanted it. How could she have forgotten? The duchy is everything, our people needed her.'

Leo's eyes glittered. 'So you hatched a plan to take power yourself?'

She'd come to terms with how Leo affected her physically, she hadn't reckoned on her prospective husband being so emotionally attentive and that he would take the time to listen and even take her seriously.

'Yes. I did. I was about to be married and that would mean losing the thing I wanted most. I had to act. If I want to truly serve the people, I have to be free.'

'Freedom,' Leo said, almost wistfully. 'That's a rare commodity indeed.'

'But you're a man and a powerful one at that. You're telling me you don't have freedom to choose?'

'The only son of a monarch, my future was mapped out for me from birth. I had no choice in the matter. How different is that from your situation?'

'Seriously? You think there's a comparison? You chose to marry Francesca and at any time you could have said no without any consequences. What choice did she or I have?'

He took her left hand and ran his thumb gently across her ringless fingers. 'And yet here you sit, having said an emphatic no. That looks like a choice to me.'

She should have tugged her fingers free but the warmth and strength of his were so comforting.

'I may have said no but you still came after me. You plan to change my mind, don't you?'

'You've already stated what you want is freedom to run the duchy yourself. I doubt you'll be persuadable.' He watched her from hooded eyes.

Her stomach did a flip. If he kept looking at her like that she might be persuaded to do anything.

But it was just a ploy to get her back on side. He might not have been responsible for the dismissal of Luisa and Rolfe, or that sudden decision for her to spend last night in Grimentz, but that didn't mean he wasn't still to be avoided. As soon as this storm cleared, he'd want her to go back to Grimentz with him and be married, she was sure of it.

She snatched her hand free and pushed to her feet.

'It's been a trying day and I'm tired. I'd like to rest for a while.'

He lounged back in his seat.

'There are two rooms in the servants' quarters we can use. Take whichever you prefer. Though if you want to bathe, now that we are without power, sadly the water will be cold in both.'

He smouldered up at her, with an added wicked curve to the corner of his mouth as he saw the blush spreading across her cheek. 'Though perhaps you'd welcome the effects of a cold shower, Grand Duchessa?'

CHAPTER SIX

LEO SAT NURSING his glass of wine.

Thinking.

Running through his various options and feeling unprepared. Because of all the reasons Violetta might have chosen to run, this was the last thing he'd expected.

A democratic duchy right on the doorstep of Grimentz? Meaning San Nicolo would be lost to the von Frohburgs for good.

His father would have been apoplectic.

Yet curiously Leo was able to summon little outrage at the prospect. A few hours ago, he'd come up here all guns blazing determined to reclaim his runaway bride. And now?

Now he was no longer sure what he wanted.

His people had their own elected bodies, with a say in how Grimentz was run. The Della Torres had not been so liberal-minded, they'd held onto power with a fierce grip. The current regent being more rigid than most. Why shouldn't San Nicolo have the same freedoms Grimentz enjoyed? He'd planned to introduce something similar once he'd become Grand Duke.

Yes, but a full-blown democracy, with potentially all power stripped from its former ruling family? That should give him pause, surely?

Again, Leo felt nothing beyond a curiosity about how that might work for the duchy.

Perhaps a pair of melting brown eyes had temporarily bewitched him?

Was that it? A woman making him think twice about what he wanted? When he'd had little cause to trust one before.

He left the kitchen and walked back through the grand hallway. With its marble pillars and elaborate chandeliers and frivolous ballroom. All symbols of the power and wealth and status of a well-connected family.

The wind had moaned and rattled at the window of her little room, but, snuggled beneath the counterpane of her single bed, Violetta had actually slept. She'd felt safe knowing that Leo was somewhere in the house, which was a revelation, because wasn't he supposed to be the last person she should trust?

The night before she'd been so tense, she'd barely closed her eyes, but now she woke feeling refreshed.

She washed her face, smoothed her elaborate

chignon and, on impulse, put the tiara back on. For some reason it gave her confidence.

On the window ledge outside her room sat a torch. Leo must have placed it there for her and she was touched by the thoughtful gesture.

The roiling clouds lashed rain against the windows, but Leo's torch lit the way as she descended the stairs of the servants' quarters.

The kitchen was cosy with its blinds drawn and storm lanterns sat on the table and dresser. The man who'd set them emerged from the pantry.

'Ah, you're up. I thought I was going to have to beat on your door to wake you.'

She rubbed her eyes. 'How long have I been asleep?'

'Several hours. It's past seven now.' He held up another of the tins from their small pantry. 'Dinner?'

'You can't already be hungry?'

'After the delights of that gruel you fed me for lunch, you mean?'

He moved around the kitchen with the same grace as he moved through his royal duties. In that collarless shirt, with his sleeves rolled back, he had such a relaxed allure about him. The dim light caught on the slash of his cheekbones, the strong jaw, those broad shoulders and lean hips.

Such a dangerous charm. She must not forget he could still so easily derail her plans for the duchy if she let him. Violetta took a steadying breath, trying to control the effect he had on her.

She watched him collect plates and cutlery and set two places at the table.

'You're actually quite domesticated,' she said, slipping into a seat.

He grasped a bottle of wine. 'You make it sound like I'm half wild.'

She watched the muscles on his forearms flex as he worked a corkscrew into its top. The strong grip of his hands as he pulled the cork clear.

How had Francesca described him? A part-tame wolf. He was all lean strength and barely contained energy. Despite their everyday sur-roundings, it was there, a distinct aura of danger. Violetta crushed her fingers together in her lap.

'I meant you seem at home in a kitchen.'

'Only this one. Grand-Mère insisted that Seb and I did our share of the chores here.'

'I used to love that. I felt like I was a regular person. Maybe like one of the servants. Able to leave all my parents' expectations behind at the end of the day.'

'We're servants too though, aren't we?' he said. 'Just not the kind who can easily choose alterna-tive employment.' Had she imagined that hint of regret? She thought he cared for nothing but power.

'Would you have liked a different career?'

He shook his head. 'My earliest memories are of my father, standing me on the castle battlements. Pointing out San Nicolo, saying that it had been stolen from us and that essentially my only reason for existing was to get it back. A different career was never an option.' He poured two glasses of wine and set one in front of her. 'Although perhaps that's where my head for heights comes from,' he said casually, as if there weren't a dark reason for that.

Violetta thought of a little boy, too tiny to see the duchy over the hulking stonework without being lifted onto it. There'd been no protective hug of a father holding a beloved son, helping him see the wonder of the world below.

More a prince drilling his obsessions into the heir. She was beginning to understand why Leo had come charging after her when she ran from the wedding.

He took a slug of his wine.

'Let's eat. I hope you're ready for the culinary adventure that is canned coq au vin?'

The table had been cleared, the dishes put away and Leo let the evening settle in over him. The violence of the storm outside forgotten, muted by the magic of this house and this night.

No one demanding his attention. Nowhere to be. Nothing to do but sit here with this woman and watch the candlelight play in her hair and glint through the emeralds of that absurdly out of place tiara.

The true magic of this house, of course, was that it made him ordinary. Just a man sharing dinner. Not thinking about tomorrow and all its implications but for the moment content to be with Violetta and enjoy her surprisingly refreshing company.

'Do you know what your castle is missing?' she asked.

'I know you're going to say a dog.'

'Yes! A big lolloping hound. I remember you and Seb tearing about the place with a dog always at your heels.'

'Yes, Grand-Mère always cared for rescue dogs.'

'You must have looked forward to seeing them every time you came.'

He shook his head. 'You know, I never came back after that summer you were here.'

'Never?' Her eyes widened. 'Why?'

'My mother left,' he said.

'And?'

He looked at her sharply. 'Surely you know the story?'

'Only the bare facts. I'd like to hear it from you.'

He almost reverted to classic Leo, sharing nothing, but those disarming liquid eyes were hard to resist.

'My mother didn't just leave, she abandoned me and my father.' And the hurt of that still had the power to take his breath way.

'So he became both parents to you?'

Leo snorted in derision. 'No. He became even less of a parent to me than he was before. He blamed me for my mother's departure. First I'd been too clingy, then not dutiful enough. It depended on the day and the mood he was in. It was always worse when news of my mother's latest affair hit the headlines. When she imagined herself in love yet again. What a futile emotion. Who needs it? So fleeting and unreliable.'

Violetta regarded him sadly, but she was in no position to offer sympathy.

'You can't pretend you've had much of it in your life either,' he scoffed.

Her gaze softened on him. 'Except for here. We were both loved here.'

'Not after I cut Grand-Mère out of my life.'

'That's not true. Right up to that last year she spoke of you with pride and affection. You were loved unconditionally by her. She even left you her beloved chateau.'

Leo recalled the regular cards and the gifts and was assailed by guilt. 'I couldn't forgive her for allowing my mother to meet her lover here and I tried to punish her for it,' he said quietly.

'You were in pain. You lashed out at the only person you could hurt because she was the only one who cared about you. She would have understood that. She was a wise woman.'

Those beguiling eyes watched him, ablaze with

certainty. It wrapped around him and warmed the cold, dead place where his heart used to be.

It was startling to realise Violetta was the first person he'd spoken to in this way. He hadn't even shared this much with Seb, but with her for some reason it felt right.

He stared at a candle guttering in one of the lanterns. 'Love is hardly top of the list for people like us.'

'Despite all the wealth and privilege, and responsibility, we are still people though, aren't we? Surely, deep down you'd want to be loved by your wife, to be happy?'

'Based on the choices I'd made about our marriage, you know the answer to that question already. In my experience it's safer to have a business arrangement with a woman from the outset, then I'm unlikely to be disappointed. A fruitless quest for happiness would only get in the way.'

She regarded him, sadly. 'But what about taking her to bed?'

'Grand Duchessa, love is not necessary for good sex, or even adequate sex that gets the job done.'

'Pregnancy, you mean? What a cold life that would be.'

'But producing an heir is vital for people like us.'

'Only if you don't believe in democracy.'

'Even then, the family won't end because it's no longer in power. There will be properties and possessions to pass down. A title to preserve.'

She huffed. 'What use is a title if you can't *do* anything with it? I know a title can draw attention to good causes, but influence can only go so far if you haven't any real power.'

He laughed at her. 'Grand Duchessa, you haven't thought this through, have you? How does that work in your world where democracy is king?'

She glanced up at him. Delighted by the sound of his laughter. 'Yes, of course, you're right.'

And why was she sharing so much? He shouldn't be this easy to talk to, he was supposed to be the enemy, but her heart ached for the boy he'd been. Trying so hard to be the man his father would be proud of and desperately hurt by his mother's rejection.

Still, she really shouldn't tell him another thing. 'I hated that I was never taken seriously.'

Oh, Violetta!

'Well, things are about to get very serious.' He checked his watch. 'In two hours, you reach your majority. You could take control as soon as you get back to San Nicolo.'

It was ten p.m.? The hours had flown in this man's company.

'Now it's nearly here I'm rather scared.' Since she became the heir to the duchy, she'd dreamed of the moment she turned twenty-one.

'When my father died, I remember feeling a combination of exhilaration and blind terror, but

I had so much work to do, there wasn't really time to think about anything but the job.'

'I was so sure before, but now suddenly I feel like I've no idea how to begin.'

'What's important to you?' he asked.

'That's easy—that people get to choose their own destiny.'

He took a lazy sip of wine. 'Well, begin there, then. Gather good people around you. People you trust, who share the same values, but who won't be afraid to tell you the truth if you're getting things wrong. Then once you have that support network in place, ask San Nicolo precisely what it wants to do.'

'You make it sound so easy.'

'It isn't, but it will be worth it.'

He was talking to her as if he believed what she wanted was possible.

'You think I can do it? Actually introduce democracy to a four-hundred-year-old absolute monarchy? Me? The girl who didn't have the guts to stand up to her uncle and say no to a marriage she didn't want.'

'Running away ten minutes before you were due to leave for the cathedral took courage. You grabbed the only opportunity you'd had at that point. Apply that to introducing democracy and you'll get there.'

'What? Run away a lot?'

'No.' He laughed. 'Grasp the opportunities as they present themselves.'

Getting naked with you and hang the consequences. That's the opportunity I want to grasp right now.

She took a gulp of her wine at that shocking thought.

Leo watched the soft blush spreading over her cheeks and wondered what had caused that. And wondered too about her ambition for herself and her duchy.

Hers was a noble aspiration. All she wanted was for her country to flourish. It had nothing to do with her needs.

How short of that did Leo's ambitions for San Nicolo come?

They were about him. His wants and his proving something to a dead man who'd never given a damn about his only son. Except for how he could benefit Grimentz. Prince Friedrich had certainly never cared about San Nicolo in the way this young woman did.

He'd let his father poison his mind and drive him in the wrong direction.

Here sat a petite woman with a big heart, caring only how she could use her position of privilege to serve others.

'What is it?' she asked, concern in those brown eyes.

What had she seen? The moment when his shame had obliterated his ambitions? San Nicolo wasn't his, it belonged to her and her people. He had no right to it.

'I was imagining you running amok in the palace of San Nicolo. Your uncle has a shock coming.'

'Uncle Guido isn't going to like this at all, is he?'

'I think that's a given.'

'Will he try to stop me?'

'Almost certainly, but you have the right of succession on your side. There is nothing in the constitution that says you can't rule. Just that you can't if you marry. Then you'd have to surrender power to your husband. But if you believe in it you should go after what you think is right.'

She smiled.

'What?'

'For a moment there you sounded just like your grandmother. She was for ever telling me to go after my dreams.'

That wasn't quite what he'd said. His comment was more cynical, less emotional. But he heard Grand-Mère's voice, too. Telling him to stop being so rigid and controlled like his father, and to lead with the heart, at least try to be happy.

She sighed. 'Imagine if my dream allowed me a husband too and it could be like this. Just two people getting to know one another, enjoying each other's company.'

Yes, he thought wistfully, just imagine…

Then dialled back. He never wanted that. That was how you got hurt.

'There are other advantages we have that others don't, which compensate,' he said.

'Like what? So far I've only experienced crushing expectation and little chance to do anything I actually want or believe in.'

'That will change tomorrow when you take power.'

'You truly believe I can do it?'

Her gaze fixed expectantly on him and he realised with some surprise that, yes, he thought she could.

'You said before that everything changed for you when Francesca ran away,' he said. 'Did you miss her? Were you close?'

'Not really. Even though we were sisters our worlds were very different. We were raised separately. She was going to marry you and be the next grand duchess. Whereas I was destined to be married off to a European aristocrat. My father said I couldn't expect the state to keep me, and that I had no other usefulness to it apart from marrying well and providing the Della Torres with wealthy, well-connected in-laws.'

Leo's anger rose at that. Another child who'd been told they had no value in themselves.

'Did it hurt you? When she ran away?' She peeked up at him, concern in her gaze. It warmed and comforted him.

'Only my pride. I didn't have any tender feelings for her, if that's what you're asking. I don't really blame her any more either. I genuinely wish her well and hope she's happy with the choices she made.'

'I hope so too. She may have been the heir but to my parents she was still just a girl. Do monarchs only love princes?' she said bitterly.

'Not in my experience.' Who'd loved him because he was the prince and heir? Definitely neither of his parents.

'Leo, I'm sorry for that,' she said, placing her hand over his.

The intimacy took him by surprise and before he could control it, all the hurt and humiliation came flooding back. Tightening his throat. He withdrew his hand from beneath hers.

'It's in the past, it no longer matters.'

'Being hurt by those who should love us always matters.'

Despite his best efforts that reverberated through him, the pain danced close to the surface again. He slammed his mind shut on it.

He didn't want this. Allowing someone close was how you got…*hurt*.

And yet this woman, with her gentle eyes and gentler hands, was creeping into the heart he'd thought was shut away for ever.

He got to his feet. 'Let's change the music.'

'Or change the subject, you mean. I get it. Talking about your feelings is painful.'

'Not at all.' With his back to her he shuffled through the collection of CDs. 'It just doesn't serve any purpose for me.'

Seb would have rolled his eyes at that one.

'Here we go again. Leo the untouchable. The man without a heart. The only person you're fooling is yourself. You're flesh and blood like the rest of us.'

Leo slammed his mind shut on that too. He found one of Grand-Mère's favourite bands and the strains of samba filled the air.

'Dance with me?' he said, stretching out his hand.

Violetta hadn't missed that haunted expression in his eyes. Despite those broad, straight shoulders, the determined chin, she'd spied it—a sudden air of vulnerability. He was briefly that teenage boy again, who'd been betrayed by both parents and had his heart broken.

She looked at that outstretched hand but couldn't trust herself to take it.

'Your grandmother used to love listening to this.' She stood and started moving by herself, swinging her hips.

'What's that you're doing?' he asked.

'It's salsa.'

'You do it well.'

'I'm a dancer, remember.'

'That's sultrier than any ballet I've ever seen.'

She swirled her hips again. 'Perhaps.'

'Teach me?'

'You can already dance.'

'Enough to twirl a visiting royal around the dance floor when required, but not like that.'

She studied him, frowning. 'How ever did you seduce all those women?'

'That's an entirely different kind of dance.' He was trying to copy what she'd just done.

Badly.

Had she found a chink in this spectacular man's arsenal? Could he really not dance?

Wooden hips. Rhythm all wrong.

Oh, Lord, badly wrong.

'Stop.' She held up a hand. 'Watch.'

She traced out a few easy steps. 'See what I'm doing. Lift your heel and your hips will move on their own.'

'What's the step called?' he asked, absolutely murdering whatever he thought it was.

'It's a cucaracha.' Her brow knotted as she watched. She took his hands in hers. 'Follow what I do,' she said. 'Yes, that's much better.' And didn't notice he'd edged closer until he gathered her up, brought their hips almost together and executed a perfectly beautiful cucaracha.

She'd have extracted herself from his arms but he'd taken her by surprise and being able to touch and feel all that strength moving beneath her fingers was intoxicating.

'*This* is how I had all that success with the ladies,' he purred.

Not with this one.

'That's enough dancing,' she said just as a slow, mellow number began.

'Come now.' He tucked her hand to his chest. 'This was supposed to be our wedding day. At least grant me our first dance. You owe me that, surely.'

A sultry songstress was crooning about losing herself to love, that it felt like home, as Leo swirled her round the room.

Oh, the man was devious. He danced beautifully. Violetta couldn't help herself, she started to enjoy it.

He twirled her out and back, and again, and this time as she danced back to him he turned her beneath his arm and then into a perfect dip. As she tipped backwards her hand flew up, grabbing his biceps in alarm, but he held her easily. She was perfectly safe, and a moment later she was upright again, being moved effortlessly round the room.

'Ready to try another dip, *la mia piccolo ballerina*?'

His little ballerina.

She shouldn't be so charmed but her giddy little ballerina heart skipped a beat. Italian spoken in that deep baritone was lethal.

So out she went, spinning beneath his arm and then back into a perfect dip. She laughed up at him, her hand resting lightly on his biceps this time, his other arm strong beneath her back.

She was expecting to come back up, but he held her there, his gaze on her mouth. Then suddenly he tightened his grip, lifted her towards him and pressed his lips to hers.

They were soft and warm and Violetta, caught off guard, let them move over hers. Her hand slid up his arm to curl about his shoulder.

He pulled her closer, deepened their kiss, and a pulse throbbed hard between her thighs.

A soft noise rolled in her throat. Her fingers on his shoulder dug in. She pressed closer so more of her body connected to his. He was all hard muscle and heat and she wanted more.

Reason, common sense, dreams and determination were forgotten…or were they? What about her people? What about San Nicolo?

Her eyes fluttered open.

It might all be lost if she allowed herself to be seduced. Distracted from the course she knew she must take.

From somewhere she found the strength to break the kiss and push him away.

Leo leant forward wanting to taste those lips again, but his met thin air. She'd lurched back in his arms and planted a hand firmly against his chest.

'That's enough of that. I know what you're planning and it won't work.'

Planning?

He'd *planned* to kiss her again, to savour the delight of her mouth and hadn't thought of a thing beyond.

She pushed at him, wriggling to get free. Reluctantly he let go.

Looking thoroughly flustered, she instantly rounded the table to put it between them. She scooped up her wine glass and knocked back its contents.

'I won't be falling for your seduction technique.' She sloshed another measure of wine into her glass and gulped that down too.

'You might want to slow down,' Leo cautioned.

'Don't tell me what to do.' She slashed an angry hand through air. 'I've had enough of men like you telling me what to do.'

Leo shrugged. 'Okay, but you may regret that in the morning.'

She sank down into a seat. 'The morning,' she said, almost wondrously. 'I'll be free. I'll be Grand Duchess, and no one will ever tell me what to do again.'

He didn't have the heart to remind her that her life was about to get a lot more complicated. Being the sole decision maker wasn't going to be the easy route.

CHAPTER SEVEN

IN ONE RESPECT Leo's wedding night was much as he might have expected. He'd barely slept.

However, that was where all of the similarities ended. He'd spent the night entirely alone, listening to the ravages of the storm outside and the restless pacing of the woman in the room next door.

More than once he'd been on the verge of leaving his room to hammer on her door and pick up where they'd left off, but he knew it wasn't the answer.

He checked his watch, seven o'clock on the day of Violetta's twenty-first birthday. She was now officially Grand Duchess and his chance at easily claiming San Nicolo had passed. Oddly, that didn't bother him as much as he'd have expected, and today was another day. If yesterday was anything to go by, who knew what it might bring? With the woman next door anything could happen and while the storm raged there was nothing anyone could do to move things along.

Despite their circumstances Leo had enjoyed his evening. Unexpected in the scheme of things.

He hadn't imagined they'd have been doing quite so much talking, expecting to be engaged in something less cerebral and more physical. But he'd liked it.

She was an excellent dinner companion, entertaining, energising. He couldn't remember the last time he'd enjoyed an evening so much.

Of course there'd be no repeat. He needed a wife. She'd declined that position and he had neither the want nor desire for a woman in any other capacity. Why would he?

A twig, torn from a tree somewhere and still bearing its lush, fresh leaves, landed with a splat against the window then was wrenched away again.

Grimentz was still in the grip of a storm. Here, in this sheltered valley, it was bad enough but what was the rest of his country suffering? While he was trapped here and powerless to do anything but wait it out.

He threw back the sheets.

He needed coffee and something to eat from their meagre pantry. Then he could put his thoughts back in order.

Who knew what time she'd finally slept? Not till the early hours at least, because she remembered a faint light creeping beneath the curtains.

Kept awake by the storm, which if anything had got worse.

But also kept awake by thoughts of the man she'd pushed away and fled from. Twice in one day.

She'd tossed and turned, she'd climbed out of bed and paced the room just to burn off some of the restless energy that coursed through her body.

She couldn't get that kiss out of her mind. Her lips burned with it and the promise of so much more from the man who was sleeping just on the other side of that wall.

Violetta grimaced. How could she have let that happen? How could she have allowed herself to… to…*want* Leo?

She ducked back beneath the covers and screwed her eyes shut for good measure. It made no difference to the fact.

She wanted Leo. His hands on her. His mouth on hers. She wanted everything he was and more.

She had not expected to like him.

Prince Sebastien, with his lazy smile and easy charm, was the likeable von Frohburg. Not stern, aloof Leo. Yet last night she'd spied a different man behind the mask, she'd caught a glimpse of his vulnerabilities. She saw his aching loss, his mistrust of women and what the bitter experience of growing up with his father had instilled in him. Along with the biting need to reclaim the grand duchy that his forebears had bred into him.

But that wasn't who he was, not at his heart. Beneath that dark facade, there was warmth and fun and kindness, if only he could allow himself to show it.

Violetta flung herself over in bed. All that should matter to her was San Nicolo and its people. Leo might have talked reasonably about her plans for radical change in her country but when it came down to it, he'd stand against it. Just as her uncle and father had. Powerful men always thought they knew better.

If she let him in then she'd be betraying all the people of San Nicolo who, like her, dreamed of a different future. Brighter, bolder, freer. Where you got to choose your own destiny. Getting tangled up with the Prince of Grimentz was a surefire way to lose all hope of that.

There was movement next door. The sound of the shower cranking on, followed by a muffled, but expressive curse as cold water hit warm skin.

Violetta couldn't help but smile.

Then the smile faded.

On the other side of the wall, in the small en-suite bathroom, His Serene Highness would be naked. Those beautiful hands working soap across his torso. That strong body sluiced with water and suds.

She'd been chilled in the night and, not wanting to explore the costume attic with its groaning timbers and in the pitch dark and moaning wind, she'd returned to the kitchen and grabbed Leo's wedding shirt from the back of a chair where he'd left it to dry.

Now she tugged the fabric closer to her nose and inhaled. It smelled of him, of his cologne. She imagined touching him, running her hands across that broad chest.

Her hands slid over her own body, along her arms, across her breasts, her belly contracted. Instinctively she clenched her thighs together. She drew the hem of the shirt higher, baring her hips, and let her fingers wander downwards over her belly, to between her thighs.

There was the rude clatter of the shower turning off, the rattle of curtain rings as it was swept back.

Violetta snatched her hand away and lay still until she heard footsteps along the landing and a heavy male tread on the stairs.

She let out a long slow breath. Time to get up herself and face him, and whatever the day would bring. But first she'd also take a bracing cold shower. It might be just what she needed to snap out of this nonsense.

Leo collected the cafetière and coffee from the pantry. Thankful the staff who visited felt fresh coffee was an essential. He was filling the pot from the tap when there was an ear-piercing scream from above.

Good God! Had someone found their way here and broken into the chateau despite the foul weather?

He pelted up the stairs, yelling for her.

'Here! Oh, come quickly.'

With fists raised he burst through the door to her bathroom. Skidding to a halt when he discovered she was alone.

Or apparently not.

'There,' she wailed, pointing to a small spider sitting in the bath.

'For God's sake, woman, I thought you were being attacked.'

'Never mind that now,' she said, hopping from foot to foot. 'Do something, please. I hate spiders!'

This was not how he'd imagined his honeymoon would be. He sighed heavily and bent down to take off a shoe, getting ready to flatten the offending creature.

'You're not going to kill it?'

'I thought you wanted it gone.'

'But you used to catch them in your hands.'

'I was thirteen and less fastidious than I am now.'

She snatched up a glass sitting on the washbasin and thrust it at him. 'Here. Use this.'

'And keep it in there how?'

She looked about her frantically, then shot out of the door. Leo heard her running from room to room.

Violetta's footsteps returned along the landing and she burst back in.

'There,' she said, handing over a piece of card. 'You can trap it in the glass with that.'

One glance at what she'd given him and his gaze shot back to hers.

'Seriously? *This* was all you could find?'

She shrugged. 'There was a pile of them sitting on a bedside table. I think someone must have had a bit of a crush.'

In his hand Leo held a postcard, the kind on sale in any principality gift shop. A photograph of him, this one had him in military uniform, looking his most pompous and austere.

With a deliberate flourish he flipped it over so his image would not be in contact with the spider. There followed a minute of undignified scrabbling about at as the intruder scuttled back and forth out of his reach. But a small arachnid was no match for a fully grown human and eventually it was caught.

Leo turned, with glass in hand, to see Violetta—the brave young woman who'd had the guts to flee her wedding yesterday—cowering against a wall, and something in him railed at the sight.

'You stand over there and Antonio and I will stand over here.' He smiled reassuringly at her.

'What? *Who?*'

'This is the famed Antonio.' He held the spider aloft. 'He needs to go back to his wife.'

She snorted. 'Spiders don't have wives.'

'Then where do little girl and boy spiders come from?'

Her lips twitched. 'So what's she called? This wife of the famed Antonio?'

'Hildegard.'

'Hildegard?' She laughed.

'Shh… He adores her and won't have anyone make fun of her.'

Violetta eased away from the wall. 'Well, that's an honourable thing, I suppose.'

'Yes, it is,' Leo said.

He and Antonio took a step towards the doorway and her. But though she kept her gaze fixed on the glass in his hand she didn't flinch as he drew nearer.

She followed him down the stairs, to the rear of the servants' wing, and the scullery door, which opened onto an enclosed courtyard, protected from the full force of the weather. Leo dropped to his haunches, carefully upended the glass beneath a rosemary bush and Antonio scuttled to safety.

As he stood, re-entered the house and closed the door back on the weather, Violetta held his gaze.

'Thank you,' she said. 'No one has ever tried to help me get over my fear of spiders before.'

'Antonio and Hildegard will be pleased they've helped you.'

'I know it's irrational. Being scared of such a teeny creature.' Her eyes clouded. 'At least that's what my father said when he locked me in a dark closet. Knowing there were spiders lurking in every corner. He said I must conquer my fears and I'd stay in there until I'd learnt to control myself. By that he meant stop crying. He left me in there for hours. I was four.' She hugged herself. Small and helpless again. 'Who does that to a child?'

'A monster, that's who!' Leo said, raging inside for her.

She gazed up at him. Her eyes filled with remembered hurt and he reached for her, wanting to clasp her to him, and eradicate all that pain, but she stepped back.

'Um…thanks.' She chewed her lip, looking torn. 'I should probably go and get that shower now.'

He watched as she hurried away. Toned, tanned legs on display beneath the shirt she wore.

His wedding shirt, no less.

He ran a hand through his hair. She'd rejected his marriage suit and after this storm abated they'd be going their separate ways. She'd no longer be his concern. She'd even just made it clear that while they were trapped here she'd prefer he stay at arm's length.

So why had he felt compelled to comfort her just now?

Because he knew intimately the pain he saw in her fathomless brown eyes and the failure of a father who'd helped put it there. And because he couldn't ignore the feeling that they shared a connection beyond being royal.

Somehow they were kindred spirits.

Thirty minutes later, in the small, first-floor room that had once been his *grand-père*'s study, Leo was perched on the edge of the desk. Long legs stretched out, ankles crossed, staring out at the view, still shrouded by rain clouds.

Out there his country was hunkered down beneath the pummelling of the storm. He could only hope that the damage was as limited as it appeared to be here. What else might await him when he returned to his castle? Would his people be angry that the duchy hadn't been restored to them or was it really just the objective of the von Frohburgs?

Was he really thinking of letting San Nicolo go? The dream that had obsessed his family for generations and his father most of all. The dream he had drummed endlessly into his only son.

'The duchy is your destiny, boy. The only reason you were put on this earth. Don't fail me. Don't fail Grimentz. Make amends for the shame your mother brought to this family.'

How often had Leo heard those words? Or something like them.

The door behind him creaked open.

'There you are.'

He glanced over his shoulder as Violetta appeared.

The temptation of her supple, toned limbs back on show in her little cheerleader dress. He couldn't be sorry. He was in sore need of cheering up as even beyond the grave his father still had the power to taunt him.

She padded towards him.

Barefoot, her chestnut hair hanging in damp tendrils down her back, she was nothing like the lofty grand duchess her birthday had made of her, or the apparently insipid woman he'd been engaged to marry. She was more vibrant and real to him than either of those illusory creatures. She hopped up beside him on the desk. Her legs swung back and forth.

'What are you doing in here?' She glanced about the room that contained only a desk, three empty bookcases and a solitary painting hanging on the wall.

'Thinking.'

She studied him, her head tipped to one side. 'About?'

'Your grand duchy.'

'You're not going to try and persuade me to marry you after all?'

'Are you persuadable?'

'No,' she said, flashing him an odd look, as if trying to convince herself as much as him. 'I won't lose the duchy by taking a husband.'

'Then I won't be wasting my time with that.' It surprised him to discover he meant it.

'But still you were thinking about it.'

'Actually, I was thinking more about what my father would say about the turn of events.' He'd have been incoherent with rage.

'He'd have been disappointed?'

'An understatement. He'll be cursing me from the grave. I can hear him now. If you don't regain the duchy what use can you be to Grimentz? You might as well have not existed.'

Violetta watched him sadly. 'Your father was a monster too.'

Long before his father's death, Leo had learned to expect nothing from him, but it didn't mean it couldn't still hurt. Like the swift stab of pain at the reminder he meant nothing but a way to grab the duchy.

'Indeed he was.'

She glanced around her. 'What room is this?'

'It used to be my grandfather's study. I regret I never knew him, but Grand-Mère kept everything as it was after he died and it was my and Seb's favourite room in the house.'

'Not because of the view?' She squinted out at the gardens lost beneath the mist and rain.

'Partly. It looks straight out over the mountains to the north. You feel like you are at the edge of civilisation and that hordes of barbarians could come streaming over the peaks at any moment.'

'Sounds lovely.'

'It was to two young boys. Grand-Père had a collection of medieval swords and shields.' He pointed at the lines of fading on the white plaster. 'They were mounted on the walls. We imagined all sorts of battles and heroics, of course.'

He fell silent for a moment. Remembering the very real, emotionally traumatic battles he'd endured back at the castle.

'Sometimes, when things with my father got really bad,' he said, 'I'd imagine climbing over those mountains and never coming back.'

'Was it often bad?'

'Yes.' His gut churned at the memories of his father's displeasure. 'However hard I tried, nothing I did ever pleased him. The best exam results, becoming captain of all the sport teams, trophies, accolades. Nothing was good enough. It got so much worse after my mother left though, as unfortunately for me I inherited her eyes. I don't think he could forgive me for being a daily reminder of her. He'd certainly never forgive me for losing the duchy.'

Violetta's conscience pricked her. Her defiance had stolen Leo's chance to finally prove Prince Friedrich wrong by regaining the duchy.

Leo caught her sympathetic gaze.

'Don't worry,' he said, with a quirk of his mouth. 'I'll move on.'

He would but not with her. She had to do this alone…didn't she?

Where had that niggle of doubt come from? Possibly because there was something so appealing about the man sitting beside her. Something about his vitality and his vulnerability. The warmth in those startling blue eyes. Not at all the prince she'd thought she'd fled from.

And then there were his kisses last night.

She peeked at him. Her gaze lingering on his

beautiful mouth, with lips that were so unimaginably soft. Her own tingled at the memory.

'Violetta,' he warned. 'If you stare at me like that I won't be answerable for the consequences.'

She blinked at him and hopped down from the desk, putting some space between them. She was far too interested in what those consequences might be and that was dangerous.

The room was empty as his father's heart had been. The only decoration left on the walls was a small canvas in a heavy gilt frame, of a young woman wearing a green brocade gown and a determined expression.

Violetta looked closer. Here was a nice neutral thing to discuss. Nothing at all tempting about fixtures and fittings.

'Who is this?'

'That's Elisabetha. At least how an artist in the sixteenth century imagined she may have looked.'

Elisabetha again. 'Who *was* she?'

'She saved Grimentz and its prince from destruction.'

'That's some feat. How did she achieve that?'

'Her father coveted Grimentz. He was more powerful, had a bigger army. He marched on the castle and lay siege to it, demanding the prince surrender. The Wolf of Grimentz refused.'

Violetta could hardly believe it. 'One of your forebears was called the Wolf?'

'He'd been badly disfigured in a fire as a child

and he'd grown up to be fierce and guarded. Where he could he avoided company, and particularly that of women.'

Could those traits be hereditary? she wondered. 'Our lonely wolf was unmarried, then.'

'Correct. But the rival king had a daughter—'

She clapped her hands together. 'Oh, there was a romance?'

He made a face. 'No. Elisabetha simply wanted to prevent all the bloodshed. One night she crept through her father's encampment, stole a horse and rode to Grimentz castle, begging admittance. The next morning when her father came again to demand the prince surrender, the Wolf stood on the battlements. With his new wife—'

'Elisabetha.' She'd taken destiny into her own hands. I knew there was a reason I liked wearing her tiara so much.'

'You know it wasn't actually hers? It's a much more recent piece.'

'Oh, don't spoil it for me.' She studied the portrait with a new respect. 'Saving the whole of Grimentz? That's quite an act to follow. No wonder my sister ran away.'

She shot Leo a glance. 'That was insensitive of me. Especially as she ran away from you here.'

'And back I had to come when you decided it was the perfect bolt-hole. I seem cursed by the place.'

'Perhaps Elisabetha is trying to tell you something?'

He snorted. 'To stay away from Della Torre women?'

'Or that you should reopen the chateau. It's a lovely old house and it deserves to be used again.'

'I'll bear that in mind,' he said, watching her with hooded blue eyes.

A wolf, she thought on a sudden lick of heat. They conjured all manner of forbidden things.

Like the tearing of clothes and fingers allowed to roam at will over naked skin.

Like being pushed back and flattened to this very desk by his big, hard body.

Her gaze slid back to his mouth and lingered there. She licked her lips. If she took a step closer, she'd be close enough to press her mouth to his. Her tempting wolf. One step.

She mustn't.

But the decision was made for her. He leant in, slid a hand to the back of her neck and drew her close.

She could have so easily resisted but she didn't. His lips were too warm and soft and every bit as inviting as she remembered. He tasted of coffee and storm clouds.

Leo's fingers massaged the base of her skull. His tongue traced the seam of her mouth. She opened hers with a sigh, letting him in. Heat curled low in the belly, a sweet, drugging heat. She lifted her hands to his chest and a growl rumbled in his throat. He wrapped a fist in her hair

and gently tugged, pulling her head back, expos-
ing her throat. He pressed his open mouth to the
pulse throbbing beneath her ear and sucked gently.

Violetta's fingers dug into his chest, her eyes
fluttered, losing focus. Dimly seeing the portrait
on the wall.

Violetta's eyes flew open.

Elisabetha stared back. Disapproving. Is this what
you really want? Think of what you might lose.

The duchy.

No.

Leo lifted his head.

'I can't, Leo.'

'They're just kisses, Violetta,' he said. 'There's
no need to look so shocked. It's supposed to be fun.'

Fun?

She stumbled back.

'Maybe to you, because what have you got to
lose if they go further? Nothing! If I let my guard
down, even for a moment, you might convince me
to marry you after all and then I'll lose everything
I've worked towards. Everything!'

She looked up at the portrait. 'I've waited so
long, put up with my father and my uncle treat-
ing me like I've no intelligence or abilities of my
own. Watched them take the duchy for granted.'

How had she forgotten?

'Men! You always think you know better. You
always take what you want and give nothing back.'

Now he was the one to look shocked, but she didn't care.

'I'm sorry but I'm not doing this.'

She took a last look at Elisabetha, who was gazing down on her in approval, Violetta hoped. Then she walked away, leaving all the temptations of the Wolf of Grimentz behind her.

Leo pressed the back of his hand to his mouth where the touch of her still burned. The floral smell of the shampoo she'd used in her hair was all around him, and the ghost of her in the pounding of his heart and the ache in his groin.

He'd lied when he'd said they were just kisses. They'd been so much more than that. No one had ever lit such a fire in his belly before.

But the anger and anguish in her eyes when she turned on him just now? He recognised that all too well. He'd seen that same look in the mirror, after every excoriating encounter with his father.

'You always take what you want and give nothing back.'

The men in her life had failed her too but perhaps, today at least, he could redress the balance and give a gift with no expectation of reward.

Something just for her, and he had the perfect idea how to do it.

CHAPTER EIGHT

SHE'D SPENT THE day avoiding him, in what was left of the library, to be precise. She told herself she'd gone to kill an hour or two reading. The history of the Grimentzian lace industry was utterly fascinating.

Really, truly it was.

But pretend as she might, some musty old book wouldn't keep her thoughts away from Leo, or kissing him, more precisely.

She had heard him wandering about the house, although mercifully he hadn't sought her out, though she'd have to face him again eventually. Maybe she was overreacting. Maybe they were just kisses after all.

Then why, amidst the shocking sizzle of energy, the explosion of heat and desire, had she felt such a connection, as if he'd reached inside her and forged a link between their hearts?

He was supposed to be the enemy, determined on wresting the duchy out of Della Torre hands. Yet he said he no longer planned to do that. What if she could trust that? What if having Leo at her side could actually be a good thing?

If he helped guide and support her, what might she achieve then? He talked to her as an equal and he'd listened to her, not dismissing her ideas and dreams for the future but actually giving advice. When had her family ever done that for her?

It was a long time since she'd trusted anyone enough to tell them what she was really feeling. She'd learned the hard way to keep her own counsel, and hug her dreams close to her heart. They'd have only ever been trampled on otherwise.

Now she wondered if he did the same. Perhaps all that aloofness was for protection and behind that cool facade beat a heart as full of hopes and crushed dreams as hers. It was a startling thought.

Another vulnerability, something to tug at your heart, something that could make you love him.

Love him?

That would have disaster written all over it. Leo had made it clear he wasn't interested in love and that was what she dreamed of. A man to stand at her side because he loved her.

Violetta stared out of the library window. Rain streamed down the other side, blurring her view of the real world beyond the walls of this house. But the real world was out there and after this storm had passed, she'd have to return to it.

This time with Leo, and the conflicting things

JULIEANNE HOWELLS   147

he made her feel would all be back in their proper perspective.

When she retreated to her room, across the single bed lay a garment bag. On top sat a note. A postcard, to be precise. On it, written in a bold hand, was:

> *Meet me at the foot of the stairs. Seven p.m. sharp. Formal attire required.*

Violetta unzipped the bag and gasped as the costume inside was revealed. Not so much costume but a gorgeous gown.

Leo had chosen something so far removed from her wedding dress as it was possible to find. A fluid, feather-covered number, screaming old Hollywood glamour. The demure neckline ran along her collarbone, the back dipped low to reveal her shoulder blades. There was even some underwear: pale pink French knickers. A jug of hot water sat on the dresser. A fluffy towel and fresh bar of scented soap sat beside it.

She was touched by all the effort he'd made for her, but what was he up to?

At seven p.m.—sharp—she approached the top of the stairs. The faux ostrich feathers on her dress shimmered as she walked. She'd left her hair down, brushed until it shone, and swept it over one shoulder. As the note had expressly said formal attire, she was wearing Elisabetha's tiara again.

Waiting for her in the hallway below stood Leo. Her foolish heart skipped a beat.

In tails and white tie, his blue sash running across his chest beneath his tailcoat, he was every girl's fantasy prince made flesh. Staggeringly handsome. She couldn't drag her eyes from his tall figure as she descended.

He paid her in kind, his gaze sweeping her from head to toe. Lingering on her breasts, her hips. The gown slithered around her, and she felt barely dressed beneath his searing gaze.

'Stunning…' he said, in a low gravelly tone. *'Tu sembre una grand duchessa.'*

'Thank you,' she said, rather unevenly. 'But I actually feel like a fairy princess.'

'So you are. I think I'm a little bewitched. I had an idea that gown would suit you but…' He waved his hand, indicating her dress. 'It's quite perfect.'

She sent him a crooked smile. 'Not at the back.' She turned to show him. 'I had to set to work with safety pins to make it fit.'

He gave the new view she'd presented a thorough appraisal.

'No, the rear view is just as ravishing.'

She flushed at his compliment. 'So we're Fred Astaire and Ginger Rogers in *Top Hat*?'

'Despite that dress I was thinking more Fred and Rita Hayworth.' He leant closer and said with his mouth against her ear. 'Because he always said she was his favourite partner.'

As warm lips shifted over sensitive skin Violetta stifled a moan of pleasure. Somehow she managed to say, 'So what's all this about?'

'Grand Duchessa, isn't it obvious? It's your birthday.' He held out an arm. 'And your celebratory dinner is about to be served.'

He'd made *dinner*? She wanted to ask from what, but her voice wouldn't work. The dashing man beside her had robbed her of her breath. His kindness now had touched her deeply. Yesterday she'd jilted him and today he'd made all this effort for her. He led her to the dining room. Where a candelabra sat on the table set for two. There was a crisp white tablecloth, the glitter of silver cutlery, the finest wine glasses and a bottle of champagne in an ice bucket.

'You found ice?'

'Once I'd taken a hammer and chisel to what was left at the edges of the freezer.' Her wayward imagination conjured a tantalising picture of him, bent over the chest freezer in the pantry, with that taut backside of his on display.

He pulled out the chair for her and saw her seated before he crossed to the sideboard and returned with a silver platter.

'Madame, this evening the chef has created something of a delicacy.' He removed the domed cover with a flourish. 'Pan-fried bread and haricots blancs in a tomato confit.'

She looked blankly at him.

'I believe in England you'd call it beans on toast,' he said. 'But do make the most of the bread. I discovered these few slices in the freezer, but the rest are spoiled. I fear we'll have to resort to more canned coq au vin for breakfast.'

He opened the champagne and filled two crystal flutes. 'This, on the other hand, is of the finest vintage.' He lifted his glass in salute. 'Thank you, Grand-Mère, for your excellent taste in wine.'

He handed a flute to Violetta, then with a formal bow and a heel-click he raised his glass to her.

'May I wish you a very happy twenty-first birthday, Grand Duchessa?'

She took a sip. Crisp, ice-cold bubbles played deliciously over her tongue.

'Good?' Leo asked as he took a sip from his own glass.

'Very good,' she answered.

She picked up her fork and started on her 'dinner'. 'How did you do all this?'

'I had a lot of free time while you were hiding away.'

'I wasn't hiding. I was educating myself about the history of the lace industry in Grimentz.'

His lips curved in a smile. 'Like I said. Hiding. What scared you most, that you liked the kisses or that you actually like me?'

She made a little harrumph and carried on eating.

'Surprised you, hasn't it?'

'The kisses? I suppose you could call them surprising as I have nothing to compare them to,' she said, spearing a single bean and popping it delicately into her mouth.

He sent her a wicked smile. 'Oh, Violetta, you really are delightful.'

She lifted her chin, 'That's Grand Duchess to you, or Your Serene Highness. Either will suffice until I decide that I like you enough to allow you to address me by my given name.'

'Then, Your Serene Highness, are you ready to move on to the next part of the evening's entertainment?'

Her gaze shot to his. In her excitement, she forgot she was pretending to be haughty. 'There's more?'

'It's your twenty-first birthday. Of course, there's more.'

When he opened the doors to the ballroom Violetta's jaw dropped.

Dozens of candles glittered in the candelabras. Dozens more bounced back from the reflections in the mirrors lining the walls. She stared up at Leo in wonder and his mouth creased in a crooked smile.

'It's your birthday and you should have a grand ball to celebrate your accession to the throne. Naturally you should be escorted by a handsome prince,' he said with a wink that made her heart race, 'and led to the floor for a dance.'

He held out his hand. She placed her fingers in his and followed him to the centre of the room.

A waltz started up. In the mirrors she caught the reflection of Leo pocketing a small black remote, and in the corner of the room spied the CD-player they'd listened to last night.

He began to move.

He held her so effortlessly, guided her so beautifully, it was easy as breathing to follow him round the room. In the flickering candlelight, they dipped, they swayed, they flowed across the floor in absolute unison, painting a masterpiece in shadows as they went. Safe in his expert hold, seduced by the music, and seduced more by this irresistible man, Violetta finally set her dancing heart free.

Suddenly his hold tightened, his steps slowed until eventually he stopped moving altogether. His eyes glittered in the dim light. The hand at her back pulled her close.

'Leo, we aren't dancing any more.'

'No,' he breathed and stopped any further observations with his mouth.

Violetta swooned, her lips clung to his, her hands grasped his lapels.

Outside the world raged, but here, together in their little world, they were safe.

He took her to a couch with its dust sheet already thrown back, and sank down on it, drawing her between his legs. His chin lifted as he reached up for a kiss. She cupped his face, the skin smooth from a recent shave. She slid her fingers into the silk of his hair, damp from his shower, and she melted at the thought of the care he'd taken for her.

She needed to touch more of him.

His jacket went first, her fingers sliding beneath the lapels, up his chest to his shoulders. He helped her, shrugging out of it, lifting up his backside to free those elegant coat tails. It landed on the floor in a heap to be instantly forgotten. Violetta was too intent on unwrapping the next layers. She unbuttoned the waistcoat, snatched at the bow tie. The studs of his shirt followed as she pulled it open and ran her greedy palms across his chest, thrilling at the quiver of his flank when her fingers found a particularly sensitive spot.

He was back on his feet, yanking at hooks and the zip and shoved trousers and underwear down his hips. He heeled off his shoes and kicked everything away.

He was even more beautiful naked. A feast for her eyes and hands. She wanted to touch, everywhere. Her gaze dropped to his erection, growing even bigger under her scrutiny. She'd have dropped to her knees and licked that fascinating bead of moisture from the tip, but with uneven breaths and trembling hands he was pulling her close again.

His hands trembled as he tugged at the fastenings of her gown and pushed it from her shoulders.

His breath was ragged as he slid the silk knickers down her hips and she stepped clear of them, her hands on his shoulders for support.

Watching this strong man unravel for her banished all Violetta's uncertainties. Being with him like this felt utterly right. She climbed onto his lap, her knees splayed wide over his thighs, and took his face in her hands and kissed him.

A new dance began, one of fingers and lips and tongues. The slide of skin on skin and a new, sensual music drowned out the other. Groans and sighs, hot, sultry words in French, Italian or indistinct, but speaking volumes nonetheless. Passion rode them both.

She was hot and wet and, oh, so needy. She wanted him inside her, all of him, because, heaven help her, there was already a piece of him lodged in her heart. She ground against him.

'Violetta, no.' Hunger and regret warred in the depths of his eyes. 'We don't have protection.' His hand slid over her belly and slipped downwards between them. 'But there are other things we can do.'

She gasped as his thumb found a sweet spot and circled.

'We'd be safe. I get my period soon,' she said, breathlessly, and rolled her hips against him again.

A ripple of excitement went through him. 'But

not like this. It's your first time. It will be too un-comfortable.'

Of course, he knew she was a virgin. The ex-amination to prove that was one of the many indignities heaped on her before their official engagement, but now her virginity felt precious. Something special to share only with him.

She moaned helplessly as his mouth went to her breast. She wrapped her arms about his head. How had she not known such delight existed? Because now it felt as if it were written in her flesh, in her very bones, just waiting for this man to unleash the poetry of desire in her. A sudden panic welled up—was this one night all they'd have? Because she wanted this in her life.

She wanted him.

Perhaps they could be lovers? As long as they didn't marry the duchy would still be hers. And that was what was important…wasn't it?

Leo caught her chin, and gently turned her face so she met his burning gaze.

'Violetta, whatever you are thinking, stop. Just feel.'

With a move as graceful and masterful as any-thing he'd executed on the dance floor, he lifted her from his lap and laid her on the couch.

His palm floated along her thigh, pushing it wider, and he moved between her legs. A wave of desire travelled over her skin.

'Just feel, Violetta,' he repeated, rising up and

taking her hips in his big hands. With one leg braced on the floor and the other bent beneath him on the couch he thrust into her. The pain was swift and sharp but quickly forgotten because Leo...

Leo was inside her. Worshipping her with the reverence of his hands and his body.

He withdrew, then gently eased into her again. His groans echoed round the room drowning out the tempest outside. His expression was a study in ecstasy.

Her arms flung back, watching this man take his pleasure in her, Violetta felt like a goddess laid out for a feast. Nothing mattered any more but Leo. So she did as he'd asked, she stopped thinking, and gave herself up to passion.

For the first time in his life, Leo wasn't thinking either.

Just feeling.

The heat of this woman, the urgent clench of her muscles around him nearly drove him over the edge.

His every instinct screamed for him to thrust, but he wanted to make this last. He wanted to watch the minutiae of every emotion chasing over Violetta's face. The wonder and the bliss, and the absolute focus.

This evening had been meant as a treat for her. And for him, a light-hearted thing to douse the heat of their earlier encounter. To make it a physical thing only and calm the emotional tempest it had unleashed in him.

Absorbed by the task of setting candles in this room, searching the costume gallery for the perfect dress, he'd almost convinced himself he'd succeeded. But when she'd appeared at the top of the stairs...

He wanted her and there were so many reasons, good, honest reasons, why he could not have her.

He touched her with extreme care, as if she might break beneath him. She felt precious, a rare treasure, almost too fine for the likes of him. The world outside might be imploding but in here, tonight, with him, she would be safe.

Later, she retrieved the ballet shoes, donned his shirt and danced for him.

As candle after candle fluttered and died and the room filled with shadows, Leo watched.

His trousers back on, but still barefoot and barechested, he sat, his legs spread wide, his arms stretched out along the chair back, and watched his fill of her.

She held nothing back, her hair flying loose as she swirled and leapt across the space.

Every sweep of her hand was like her touch across his skin. Leo felt it to his core as if she danced through his soul. The arabesques, the leaping splits, the strength of her supple body, he wanted to cleave it all to him. He watched as she danced, then laughed and goofed around, until he couldn't stand not touching her and went to her.

He closed his hands about her waist. She sank against him, kissed him like the angel she was, and a storm of longing, wild as the chaos outside, surged through him. A need to capture this moment and keep a piece of it with him for ever.

Because he knew these hours, as impermanent and insubstantial as the guttering candlelight, were all they could have.

CHAPTER NINE

LEO WOKE TO a strange new sensation.

A woman in his arms, deeply asleep. Her head tucked beneath his chin, her hair across his chest, her legs tangled in his.

On the floor beside the couch the scatter of clothes told its own story. The iconic dress was a forgotten pile of feathers. His waistcoat, shirt and trousers lay in a heap, and, feet away, his bow tie, flung there by this woman's hands.

His arms were wrapped protectively around her. His sleeping self had wanted to hold her… his waking self was also loath to let go.

Leo drew her closer.

But the world beyond the ballroom was intruding, because the storm had finally blown itself out, allowing other sounds to reach him. Feet on the gravel close to the house. The voices of his security team calling instructions back and forth, a helicopter approaching.

Leo lay there, not moving, wanting to preserve this moment for a little longer. To pretend he lived in a world where he and Violetta could both have what they wanted.

He turned his cheek against her hair.

Impossible, but also for the best.

The storm had passed both inside and out and he'd weathered them both. This…whatever it was…was done. He might have taken her virginity, but he wouldn't be taking her grand duchy.

He couldn't. It would be morally wrong and, despite what his father had wanted, Leo finally understood he'd never truly be that man and he was glad of it.

Friedrich von Frohburg had been a tyrant, coveting the grand duchy for all the wrong reasons.

Leo would not be so heartless. He let go of that dream.

Now there was another to let slip away.

He shook her gently. Violetta stirred, looking up at him with luminous, trusting eyes. The breath caught in his throat.

'We need to get up,' he said, eventually. 'They're coming for us.'

Through a gap in the shutters Violetta watched the helicopter touch down on the lawns, its fuselage resplendent with the scarlet and gold of the von Frohburg coat of arms. It was a great shiny beast, big enough to seat twelve in luxurious comfort. Rivalling any used by the most powerful leaders on the planet.

The Della Torres were rich, but they had only

one small private jet at their disposal. Violetta knew this helicopter was only part of the von Frohburgs' royal fleet. It was a compelling physical representation of their power.

How easily they could swallow up San Nicolo, but they could also support it and help it to grow.

A new future was possible. One where a man *could* stand by her side, as her lover, as her equal. Violetta felt a surge of excitement, of confidence. Whatever difficulties her uncle was about to throw her way, if she had Leo to lean on and lend her his strength she could achieve anything.

The steps of the helicopter lowered and Seb appeared.

Violetta watched as Leo approached, crossing the gravel with his long, powerful stride. Even dressed in last night's creased shirt and crumpled black trousers he was still the quintessential alpha male.

Tender, well-loved muscles pulsed in recognition. He was her mate. Just looking at him rocked her to her toes.

A second figure emerged from the helicopter and Violetta's brow creased. San Nicolo's former prime minister was here?

Signor Carello had been dismissed when her parents died and Uncle Guido had assumed the regency. Her uncle had cited poor governance as the reason at the time, though his evidence had been flimsy at best.

If he was here now and her uncle was not, then something serious had happened.

What had Leo said? Find good people who share your values to work with. Signor Carello was one of those. He'd always taken time to listen to her, answered her questions, taken her seriously.

As far as she knew she was now Grand Duchess, which she'd claimed she'd wanted more than anything. Time to step up and take responsibility. Perhaps she could start by working with this man.

She tugged on her wedding shoes and that feathered beauty of a dress and, because it was probably the worst outfit for such an occasion, she pulled on Leo's tailcoat to add a sombre note. It swamped her but at least it made her look less frivolous.

She combed her fingers through her hair and twisted it down over one shoulder. She left the house and headed towards the men. Their expressions altering as they saw her. The one she enjoyed most was Leo's. His warm gaze rested on her until she arrived at his side.

Seb was the first to greet her.

'Grand Duchessa, may I say how very lovely you look this morning?' He took her hands and lifted each in turn to his lips.

From Leo came an odd, low growl, which seemed to amuse Seb enormously. Leo simply glared at him.

She freed her hands and offered one to Signor Carello, who bent low over it.

'Your Highness, we are most relieved that you are safe and well.'

'Thank you, Signor Carello. Forgive me, I'm confused. Where is my uncle?'

He sent a speaking glance to Leo, who gave a brief nod.

'Tell her everything,' he said. 'She's the grand duchess now. She needs to know what's happened.'

'Ma'am, I apologise for my unannounced arrival but I have some shocking news.'

First, he said, she should be reassured that, unlike Grimentz, which had suffered significant and devastating damage, San Nicolo had been spared the brunt of the storm.

Violetta's gaze flew to Leo's. His expression grim, he merely nodded for Signor Carello to continue.

In the grand duchy there was minor damage, a few flooded vineyards, power lines down, but there was more to tell. Much more and every bit as catastrophic as if the storm had done its worst.

Violetta listened in growing shock.

The moment her uncle knew her wedding to Leo wasn't going ahead he'd fled the country. He'd been counting on the marriage to refill the San Nicolo coffers that he and her father had emptied. Oh, not through any malice. While it would have increased their personal wealth, they'd thought to make the duchy as rich as their neighbour. But their investment plans had been high risk. Her father had been weak and allowed himself to be persuaded by his younger, more ambitious brother, who'd continued on the path after the grand duke's death. The investments had failed. That was why he was so keen for his younger niece to make the match with Leo.

San Nicolo was flat broke.

Marry me, Leo thought. *Marry me and I can make all those problems go away.*

He could legitimately pour funds into the grand duchy, but then she'd be bound by her constitution, which would immediately hand all power over to him. She'd lose all chance of running the country herself. Her dreams of democracy would be over.

If they remained apart he could not fund San Nicolo's recovery without it appearing as if he were trying to take the duchy by stealth. He would be unable to offer anything but the most basic financial support.

There was no choice, he had to let her go, and could offer nothing in the way of help. A steel gauntlet clamped about his heart.

Violetta was speaking.

'I have my personal wealth. We have the family treasures. We can raise the funds we need to fund the essential services in the short term and we'll take it from there. I won't let the people suffer because of my uncle's reckless behaviour.'

Dressed in baby-pink feathers and a man's tail-coat that swamped her, dwarfed by the three men towering over her, she was still every inch the grand duchess.

It was hard to say who looked the most surprised at this new, determined Violetta: her minister or Seb, who shot his cousin a look. Who *was* this woman?

Leo's chest swelled in pride, but his moment had also passed. She'd already laid out her plans and none had any mention of him.

The shaft of pain was quickly bested. How was it any different from anything he'd been hurt by before? His own mother hadn't loved him enough to stick around. His only value to his father had been as a pawn to reclaim the duchy. With a bitter taste in his mouth, he acknowledged he'd even failed in that.

In comparison, rejection by this woman was trifling.

He'd survived before and he'd get over this... this...infatuation, surely, it was nothing more than that. A man did not fall in love in two days. It was the circumstances they'd found themselves in. None of the attraction he felt would survive being back in the real world.

She gazed up at Leo, those warm brown eyes filled with compassion. And some newly tender thing inside him cracked apart. 'But first we help Grimentz,' she said.

She was moving on, so must he.

'Then we'd better get on with it,' he said.

Leo beckoned towards the helicopter. Two more figures appeared. Matteo, Leo's valet, bearing a small suitcase and, behind him, a woman, also clutching a bag.

'Luisa...' Violetta breathed. Her dresser, her *friend*. She wanted to run to her and fling herself into her arms, but she was mindful of the men around her. She was a grand duchess now.

Leo gazed down on her, gauging her reaction, and she knew who she had to thank for the restoration of her closest confidante.

'Thank you,' she mouthed as Luisa arrived at her side with a curtsy.

Leo dipped his head in acknowledgement.

'Can you have your mistress ready to leave in ten minutes?' he asked.

'Of course, sir.'

Precisely ten minutes later Violetta, in jeans and blue shirt, was climbing into the helicopter. She'd avoided all the questions Luisa's eyes had asked but the woman had mercifully left unvoiced.

'Later,' Violetta had said, not able to tell her the truth of what had happened.

The man I ran away from is stealing my heart.

Leo joined them, in jeans and heavy boots.

As the helicopter lifted into the sky Violetta watched the chateau disappear beneath her. Apart from some missing tiles and fallen trees it was relatively undamaged. A place of magic still.

She wanted to take Leo's hand but he was on the opposite side of the cabin. Even if she could, she doubted he'd notice. His whole attention was focused on the view below.

Beneath them Grimentz lay in ruins.

Fields had become lakes, barns were flattened, mighty trees upended like saplings. In the village streets, cars bobbed like children's toys in the angry, roiling water filled with all the debris swept up in the deluge. Power lines down, bridges nothing more than archless stumps, stranded in the swollen rivers.

There was damage everywhere, even the road from the city she and Leo had both taken to the chateau just forty-eight hours ago was washed away in three places.

The devastated landscape echoed the financial catastrophe awaiting her when she returned home, but she wouldn't think of that right now. Her first priority was to help those in need in Grimentz.

They landed on the outskirts of a small town, where Grimentz had been hit the hardest. West of the capital and directly in the path of the torrents of water funnelling down the once picturesque valley. It was unrecognisable from the place it had been.

The council offices had been spared and turned into a makeshift refuge for bewildered families to gather, to get help, to enquire for loved ones.

When they saw Leo, his people fell on him, thanking the fates that he'd been spared.

They all wanted to touch him, as if to check he was real. They shook his hand, patted his back. An elderly matriarch struggled up from her seat, placing a hand to his jaw and kissing him on the cheek.

He bore it all, though Violetta could see how it moved him. He spoke with each of them, a smile for some, a handshake for others, crouched on his haunches to talk gently to a tiny girl clutching a mud-splattered teddy.

Here was another Leo. Not stern and unapproachable, but at ease amongst his people and well beloved by them in return, she realised as she watched the little girl step into his arms for a hug.

Violetta fought back a tear.

For her there were odd looks, glances at her ringless left hand, bemusement as to why she was there at all with their prince after their botched marriage attempt. Not recrimination exactly, for who would dare with their prince standing by?

Something bumped into her back, a woman entering the building struggling with boxes piled with blankets and clothes.

Her eyes went wide when she saw who she'd walked into.

'I'd curtsy, Your Highness, but as you can see…' She adjusted her grip on the boxes. 'I'd struggle with this lot.'

'Let me help you.' Violetta took one off the pile. 'Where is this going?' The woman tipped her chin towards to the side of the hall where trestle tables had been set up and volunteers were busy sorting through piles of donated clothing and bedding.

Violetta dumped her box with the stack waiting to be sorted, then rolled back her sleeves.

'What can I do?' she asked the team working round the tables.

For a moment she thought her offer was going to be refused. All the volunteers just stared at her. Some even looked openly suspicious and she couldn't really blame them. Not only was she a reviled Della Torre but the second one to very publicly jilt their prince.

The woman who'd delivered the boxes saved her, pointed at the line of four tables in turn. 'Children's clothes. Women's. Men's. Bedding and towels go on the last one.'

Smiling at her fellow volunteers, two of whom at least now smiled back, Violetta picked up the first box of donations and, with Luisa at her side, started sorting.

Leo had deliberately sat on the opposite side of the cabin so he couldn't reach for her, because he'd known how much he'd want to.

As the horrors had been revealed below he'd badly wanted to curl his fingers through hers and take strength from the warmth of her slender fingers in his.

Instead, Leo stood alone. That was what a leader did. Showed no weakness, no vulnerability and you certainly didn't hold a woman's hand for comfort.

So he'd stayed on the other side of the cabin so

he wouldn't indulge his yearning, reveal his *weakness*, and reach for her.

She'd made no fuss when the news of her country's financial ruin had been revealed. She'd listened and then turned all her attentions to helping Grimentz, whose need right then was greater. Then she'd sat, drawn but composed, as she'd stared down on what the forces of nature had wreaked on his country. When his people had eyed her with suspicion at the relief centre, she hadn't faltered, she'd simply rolled up her sleeves and started helping.

His brave girl.

She'd grown in stature before him, bearing little similarity to the girl who'd fled their wedding.

On the other side of the room now he could see she'd started directing the deliveries of new donations. They were coming in thick and fast and their current system for processing was close to being overwhelmed. She'd seen that, stepped in and reorganised it. His people didn't appear to mind, just hurrying to do as she asked.

She was doing what she claimed she'd wanted, being a leader. Being a grand duchess.

Perhaps he had a bigger job for her than this single relief centre.

The woman taking a new box from Violetta's hands suddenly dropped into a curtsy. Leo stood beside her. He took Violetta's elbow and ushered her to a quiet corner.

'The next village needs our help,' he said. 'We're going up there with the helicopter to help in the evacuation. Would you mind if I send you back by road? It's safe from here back to the city.'

'Of course,' she told him.

His smile was all relief. 'Then can I impose on you further? In his country's hour of need my cousin, and illustrious heir, has taken to his rooms and is refusing to come out. Will you represent me at the relief efforts at the castle instead?'

She blinked up at him, moved by this mark of trust in her.

'Of course,' she said, a little unevenly. 'It's what I've been trained to do after all.'

'Thank you.' He squeezed her hands. 'Before you go, I'd like you to meet Tomasz and Pierre.' He beckoned two men over. 'They're your body-guards until you can appoint your own. Tomasz you almost know. He's fond of basking.' Leo sent her that crooked smile of his. The kind that could make a girl agree to almost anything.

'Do I really need—?'

'This one's non-negotiable, I'm afraid, Grand Duchessa. You're our guest and I'll have you pro-tected accordingly. These men will guard you with their lives. I would not put someone so precious in their care if I didn't know that for a certainty.'

She wanted to keep Leo at her side for longer. She wanted to feel his strength and certainty as she took her first faltering steps into being a monarch. What a surprise to discover that having him in her life wasn't stifling at all, but freeing.

He was already moving away, taking his own entourage of security with him. She felt better seeing the muscled figures flanking their prince.

'Ma'am?' Basking Tomasz held a side door open for her and outside waited three cars and more security. Leo had already disappeared or she might have challenged him on that.

When she arrived at the castle that newfound confidence faltered as a member of the castle staff approached her.

She was grateful to have Luisa and Tomasz at her side, and Pierre at her back, as the woman arrived.

'Your Serene Highness,' she said on a quick curtsy, 'I'm Helene. Head of the Household. The prince called ahead. We will be grateful to have your help.'

Violetta stiffened her spine. She wouldn't let Leo down, or the people of Grimentz. Not in their hour of need.

This was what she'd been trained to do: to support. She did it now.

'The press are here, I'm assuming?'

'Yes, ma'am.'

'Then I'd like to speak to them.'

CHAPTER TEN

THIRTY MINUTES AFTER her press conference the
people of San Nicolo began arriving. It was a
trickle at first but soon it was hundreds, who gathered up supplies as they went and packed into
boats to make the short, but perilous trip across
a lake swollen with flood water and storm debris.
Answering the call of their new grand duchess
and coming to the aid of their stricken neighbours
regardless.

Doctors and emergency personnel of course,
but so too had come the teachers, the pastry chefs,
the vintners, and every able-bodied person in between. The castle courtyard was filled with them.

Her head of exports was soon organising the
relief effort coming from the duchy and liaising
with his opposite number in the principality. Helping bedraggled and shocked Grimentzians who'd
fled their homes and sought shelter in the capital.
Her finance minister was coordinating the supplies coming up from the lake. The mayor and his
team were ferrying Grimentzians across the lake

to stay in the hotels, guest houses and even private homes, and countless ordinary citizens were pitching in. Some even just handing out hot drinks from flasks they'd brought with them.

Violetta couldn't have been more proud or more moved when they saw her and fell on her in delight. No recriminations for having run away, just relieved to find her safe and well.

She liaised with the wider relief efforts and the teams out in the countryside, expediting decisions that normally would have required Leo's approval. She acted as spokesperson for the press. She buoyed up exhausted volunteers. Even scooped up small children from weary parents, giving the adults a moment to catch their breath while she entertained their little ones.

From some there were odd looks at finding themselves greeted by the grand duchess of San Nicolo, but this was what she'd been trained to do. Create order for the staff and charm the populace. And she did it well.

For hours.

Only once she knew everyone was settled, the last of the homeless found temporary accommodation, the exhausted staff sent to their own beds and a team in place to cover any stragglers, did Violetta ask Helene to show her to a room she and Luisa could use.

Violetta assumed she'd be back in the small room she'd fled from, but it was a thing of the

past. Instead, she was taken to the suite desig-
nated for the crown princess.

The Elisabetha Suite, Helene told her.

Of course it was.

His mother's old apartments, and every consort that had gone before her. Perhaps even the
famed Elisabetha herself—this part of the castle
was old enough.

They would have been Violetta's too had she
married Leo.

'I think there's been a mistake—'

'No, ma'am. The prince was most insistent.'

The rooms were stunning, in blue and gold,
with elegant gilt-edged furniture and soaring ceil-
ings. Violetta had always lived in luxurious comfort, but never such splendour. Behind her Luisa
whistled softly at the vast windows where pale
blue drapes hung down in voluptuous folds caught
up by lavishly embroiled swags. As for the bed,
it was enormous, with a crown all of its own,
perched high overhead and draped with more op-
ulent swags of blue silk.

Piled high with downy pillows and a sumptu-
ous silk eiderdown, it was a bed made for so much
more than sleeping and with more than enough
room for two.

Luisa caught her eye and raised a brow.

Violetta blushed and turned her attention elsewhere.

In the centre of the room sat a table with a vase

of flowers. From the mass of gorgeous yellow roses, a postcard peeked out.

One of *those* postcards.

In this photo Leo was in mid-manoeuvre, perched on the edge of dinghy racing through a choppy ocean, doused by the waves, his gaze focused intently on the horizon. On the reverse, in his now familiar hand, and anticipating precisely the objections she'd had, he'd told her he'd not hear of her staying anywhere other than this suite. He was not about to insult a fellow monarch who'd brought her entire country to the aide of his in its hour of need.

It was the postscript that really warmed her heart because that was for her, Violetta, and not the grand duchess.

I thought you'd enjoy this one. I'm looking particularly macho, don't you think?

Despite her weariness, that raised a smile.

Macho and hot. Her heart gave a flutter.

In the midst of everything he'd faced as leader of a devastated country, he'd found time to write this postcard and show such tenderness and caring.

Violetta's heart fluttered again. Did he *really* care for her?

Did he love her?

Somehow despite all his self-assurance she

knew that he was scared too. As was she, terrified that he could so easily crush her fragile heart.

Neither of them had known much love in their lives, growing up with parents who'd failed to provide even the most basic of affections. She doubted he'd be able to make that first step.

She would just have to be brave enough for both of them.

She showered, then dressed in the ivory silk nightgown and lace peignoir that Luisa had supplied with a knowing smile before disappearing for the night.

Then Violetta settled down to wait.

For every question he'd asked, 'the grand duchess' had been the answer.

Who had spoken in the numerous press conferences to ensure the help it so needed came pouring into his country?

Who had seen to it that the palace staff had been fed and replaced by her own people when they'd clearly done enough?

Who'd made decisions and kept their spirits up all day?

He could see his staff had been impressed.

In her own moment of extreme crisis, she stood by his side.

Her people and his mixed together, working side by side for the first time in four centuries.

Disaster would do that to a country. Grimentz had been offered help and accepted it gratefully.

The people of San Nicolo forgetting any enmity and discovering ordinary human beings populated the towns and farms of their neighbour. All day he'd seen it. Teams of rescue workers from both nations, wading through the floodwaters, rescuing those trapped in flooded homes. Handing them over to the volunteers who'd been more fortunate and whose homes were now thrown open to those in need. San Nicolo farmers helping their neighbours ferry terrified animals to safer pastures.

He'd been told that boats had been going back and forth all day to San Nicolo. Bringing supplies in and ferrying refugees back to the hotels and guest houses and homes of their neighbours.

The lines had been blurred. Trust and mutual respect had won the day.

His tiny grand duchess had worked wonders.

He knew he shouldn't be doing it even as his weary feet took him up the stairs and to the suite of rooms he'd insisted she have for the night. But he had to see her. One more time, before he let her go for good. He wanted her to have her duchy, to have her dream. What he felt for her was messy and emotional and he didn't do either. It had never been what he wanted. He didn't want to *feel*. It was too painful.

He made a deal with himself: he'd only knock on her door if it was obvious someone was still up.

A sliver of light spilled beneath the door.

If a servant opened the door, he'd ask for his thanks to be conveyed to her mistress, then say his goodnights and retire to his own bed and that would be the end of it.

But if Violetta answered his summons herself…?

He lifted his hand and rapped out a brief knock.

It was after one when she heard the knock on her door.

Braced with a hand on the wall, mud-splattered and bone-weary, Leo swayed on the other side.

He followed the direction of her gaze, dropping to take in his mud-stained clothes.

'I'm sorry. Perhaps I shouldn't have come.'

'Yes, you should,' she said, taking his hand. 'You are in precisely the right place.'

She drew him across the threshold, closed the door behind him, locking out the world, and brought him safe into the domain of the princess consort.

Elisabetha would have been proud of her.

'I've heard about all that you did for us today. I've come to say thank you,' he said.

'It seems paltry in light of everything the people have gone through.'

'Don't underestimate the impact you've had. My team here are full of praise.'

She hugged his praise to her. 'Then I'm glad I was here and able to help.'

He sank down on the edge of a sofa.

'How bad was that village you went to?'

'Much worse than the one you saw,' he told her. 'Every home was destroyed. We rescued a young couple and their children. They were clinging to an outhouse rooftop when we found them. That was all that was left of their farmhouse. Their family had lived in it for generations and in one night they lost everything.'

'You being there would have been a great comfort to them.'

He snorted in derision. 'What comfort could I bring in the face of all that?'

'Immeasurable' she said softly. 'I saw how your people were with you in the rescue centre. They hung on your every word…they love you.'

He sank his head into his hands.

'How do you comfort family after family who've lost their homes? Business owners whose entire life's work is gone in one night? It was a miracle that no one died.'

'Start there, then,' she said. 'Lives have been spared. The rest can be rebuilt and you'll make that happen.'

He ran a weary hand across his brow. 'I kept thinking, what would my father have done?'

'None of the things you did today. None of the

things that people really needed. Grimentz is fortunate they have you now and not him.'

He looked up at her. 'You sound so certain.'

'I am, Leo. You're a good man and a good leader.'

'Today it seemed like nothing I did was enough.'

For that moment this strong, vital man looked defeated and she couldn't bear it.

'Have you eaten?' she asked him.

'No, but don't disturb the staff.'

'There's no need to.' She pointed to a trolley with covered platters on it. 'I had something put ready for you, just in case.'

'You're a marvel,' he said.

'If I am it's my mother's doing. She may not have loved me and my sister, but she made damn sure we'd be useful.'

'I'm sorry for that. I know what it is not to be loved.'

Another truth, another vulnerability to chip away at her heart.

'Your people love you.'

He glanced up. 'You sound surprised.'

'No, I'm impressed. My father and uncle never tried to earn that love. They thought it was theirs by right. They could never have done what you did today. I saw you give so much of yourself.'

'It's just part of the royal act.'

'No. It's what you are. You cared about those people. You couldn't pretend about that. I saw that old woman touch her hand to your cheek.'

She mimicked the gesture, placing her palm against his jaw. Weary blue eyes gazed up at her.

'I'm filthy,' he warned.

She bent and pressed a soft kiss to his lips. 'Then let's get you clean.'

Heat flared in his eyes as she urged him to his feet and took his hand. He let her lead him to the bathroom and stood meekly while she turned on the shower, gathered towels. She came to stand before him. Aware of his intense blue gaze tracking every move. She unbuttoned his shirt. She reached her arms about his waist to tug it from his waistband and pushed it from his shoulders.

She knelt at his feet to untie the mud-caked laces of his boots and waited as he heeled them off and bent to remove socks.

She rose up as the steam gathered around them.

A tug at the heavy buckle of his belt drew a sharp intake of breath from him. She loosened it then wrestled with the stiff metal button of his jeans. She lowered the zip over the growing bulge at his crotch. She pushed the jeans and underwear down over his lean hips. He shoved them down the rest of the way himself, stepped clear and kicked them away.

The knot on her wrap was loosened and the whole thing fell to the floor in a whisper of silk. She tugged the nightgown over her head and dropped that too. Such a pretty thing to discard but the heat in Leo's gaze as it slid over her body was compensation enough.

She caught up her hair in a clip, then took Leo's hand and led him beneath the water. She picked up soap and a sponge and worked up a lather. She swept it across his arms and shoulders, over that broad chest, the flat abdomen.

She handed him a bottle of shampoo and waited while he washed his hair and sluiced the suds away and tried to control her breathing as she watched him, a need clawing along her spine and pooling as molten heat between her thighs.

She stepped behind him, to soap his muscled back, the deep cleft between his buttocks, the vulnerable skin of his inner thighs.

She anointed his feet with the sponge, his shins, the backs of his knees.

He turned, his erection jutting upwards. She bathed him there too, her hand massaging through the mat of hair surrounding it, before sliding along the shaft. She pressed her thumb in a circle around the tip, revelling in his fractured breath. She'd banished the defeat and weariness there had been in his eyes when he'd arrived at her door. There was only hunger and heat in their hooded depths now.

It wasn't meant to feel this way, it was just supposed to be physical. A way to ease the tension riding him. Not something that shook his heart.

Leo trembled with every touch of her fingers. They seemed so sure, so steady.

He felt as steady as a skiff tossed on a raging ocean.

Her fingers squeezed around him and he moaned. It echoed off the tiled walls and came back at him through the steam. She held him firm and he wanted it to last for ever.

As she worked him she pressed her mouth to his chest, grazed a nipple with sharp white teeth. He groaned again and wrapped his fingers in her hair and tugged to tip her face up to his, to kiss her, trying to claw back some control because he was fast losing what little he had.

Throughout all that had happened today, over and over he'd thought of this. Being with her again. He was usually a generous lover but right now there was just a raw, selfish longing to see passion kindled in her brown eyes and watch them melt to rich, dark chocolate. To feel those supple legs clamped about his waist, as her body rode his. Demanding pleasure from him and sending him into wild oblivion.

For tonight—and he knew it had to end tonight—to forget everything and just be with her.

With one step he'd pinned her against the tiled wall. Then he lifted her, thrust into her. Sank to the hilt so there was nothing but heat and lust between them.

Her gentle lover was gone.

There was no tenderness, no care, but Violetta didn't want it.

She didn't want the urbane prince, she wanted the man, stripped of his veneer of royal restraint and at his most elemental.

He'd come to her, needing her. She dismissed any notion it was because she was conveniently there. That wasn't the look in his eyes when she'd opened the door to him.

She'd drawn him in. She'd led him here, to this moment, to the lash of passion and hunger and a flaying need to prove they were alive and whole. After all they'd both seen that day, the devastation, the terrible loss, they needed to feel *alive*.

The water sluiced away the suds and the dirt, washing them both clean. Their hands on each other, their bodies joined, making them new. Blurring the edges of the pain, the images of suffering they'd witnessed.

Easing the endless pain of those deeper hurts and betrayals by those who should have loved them and hadn't.

In this moment they'd become each other's soul mate. It was them against the world.

Violetta's heart flowered opened, the last of her defences fell, and she let him in. Gave him everything, holding nothing of herself back.

'I love you,' she said. 'Oh, God, Leo, I love you.'

She came around him on a cry.

Still buried deep inside her, he stepped from the

shower, grabbing towels to fling beneath them as he laid her on the tiled floor.

Before her eyes the prince was unravelling and the man he tried so hard to hide emerged. Almost savage and never more beautiful than now, when she was his sole and absolute focus. On his knees between her thighs, his hands clamped about her hips, he pounded into her. The corded muscles of his neck grew tighter and tighter, his gasping breaths more frantic.

Then on a roar of completion, he flung back his head and spilled himself inside her.

Violetta lay there, her heart pounding, briefly unable to summon any strength to move.

On his knees still, breathing hard, Leo shoved an unsteady hand through his wet hair. Rivulets of water ran down his heaving chest and abdomen and disappeared into the crisp dark hair around his sex.

He slid out of her and stood, grabbed a towel, hitching it about his waist. He took her hand, helped her to her feet, wrapped her in a bath robe. Took a fresh towel and carefully squeezed the excess water out of her hair.

He tenderly pushed a stray damp lock from her brow, pressed his lips there instead. 'Now I need that food you promised me,' he said, taking her hand.

She went with him back into the lounge and watched as he sank to one of the armchairs.

She removed the covers from the food trolley. Her fingers trembled as she scooped sliced meats and cheese onto a plate. There were olives and bread from Grimentz and a bottle of San Nicolo wine. She poured two glasses.

He waited, bare chested, bare legged. Unselfconsciously sitting there and making no comment on what she'd just declared.

She handed him the plate and a napkin. Set the wine on the small table beside him. She bit her lip.

'Did you hear me?'

'I heard you, Violetta.'

'And?'

He made her wait while he ate some of the bread and olives, sipped his wine.

'And it changes nothing. We've had this conversation before, remember. It's not possible for people like us. The sooner you accept that, the sooner all the madness and striving goes away. Be the leader your country needs. That's what you were put here to do and there's satisfaction to be had from that.'

What about the satisfaction they'd given each other just now? Wasn't that also a precious thing?

'But I want you, too.'

'That's not possible.'

'Why not? I love you,' she said. Oh, it felt so right to say that out loud. She knew it now. That was what all the conflicting emotions of the last few days had been about. 'With everything I am, I love you. How can you pretend that doesn't mean anything for us?'

There was a long pause.

'You'll love your duchy more, trust me. Nothing will come close. Certainly not me.'

How could he believe that after the way she'd just given herself to him? Was he made of stone?

'You're saying I can't have both. I'm a woman first and a princess second. San Nicolo can have my days, but my nights… They'd be for you.'

'You're being naive, Grand Duchessa. San Nicolo will swallow you whole. You'll belong to it entirely and you'll have nothing left to give.'

Her fingers tightened around her wine glass. 'You're rejecting me?'

'I'm just being realistic. You'll have to trust me on this. Accept I have more experience and know what I'm talking about. It just couldn't work, Violetta. Two monarchs with impossible workloads. Overcommitted already. What time would we have for each other?'

Why did all that feel like a lie?

'You were prepared to marry me before.'

'When you were to be my consort, with very different responsibilities.'

Or before he got to know her and developed feelings for her. She gathered her courage. It was now or never. She took a step closer to him.

'You're scared.' His eyes flashed in warning but there was too much at stake for her to back down. 'You're scared that you'll get hurt. That your heart will be broken all over again. You must know I'd never do that.'

'It has nothing to do with my heart and everything to do with the practicalities of the situation. You have no idea what it's going to be like once you take on your responsibilities.'

Her shoulders tensed. 'A man telling me he knows better. How many times have I heard that before? I'm not stupid. I may not have had much responsibility yet, but of course I know what will be expected of me as monarch will be a stretch. But I'm strong and I'll do what it takes.' She began to pace.

'Violetta, see sense. I've been doing this for years. I know what I'm talking about.' He was still but his eyes tracked her movements back and forth.

'I won't accept that we can't follow our hearts on this.' Her own was beating hard. She had to make him see. She couldn't lose him.

'Follow *your* heart, you mean. I don't agree with your assessment of our situation.'

'Situation?' She stopped dead in front of him. 'It's love, Leo. Love! And I think you feel the same.'

He stood, wiped his hands on the napkin and dropped it beside his empty plate. 'If that's what you believe, Grand Duchessa, then you're doomed to be disappointed.'

So cynical, and she knew to the bottom of her soul he was wrong. Yes, his heart had been twisted and broken by what his parents had visited on him, but he wasn't as stone-hearted as he pretended. How could she prove that to him?

'What will it take to get past the barriers you've put up in here?' She pounded a fist on his chest.

'There's nothing in there to find.' He gazed down his nose at her. Unmoved.

'I know that's not true. I know there's a beating heart in there. I've heard it.' She pressed her body up against him. 'I've made it beat faster.'

'That's just sex,' he said. But she felt the ripple of energy go through him. He wasn't as calm as he pretended.

'Is that why you knocked on my door tonight? Just for sex.'

'Yes.'

The pause had been infinitesimal, but she'd heard it all the same.

'You're lying. Not just to me but to yourself. You feel something for me. Admit it. Let the man be free for once and not the prince.'

'Violetta,' he growled in warning. 'After all I've seen today, trust me, you don't want to unleash the man.'

'That's exactly what I want. Can't you get it into

your thick skull? I never wanted the prince. But now I know the man, he's what I want.'

'He's not available. You could have had the prince, but you made your decision about that when you ran away from our wedding.'

'So that's it? You *are* rejecting me.'

'I'm making the wiser decision for both of us.' He threw a glance to the bed, then back to her, his dark gaze all heat and need. 'But we still have what's left of tonight. Let's not waste it.'

'That's all you'll give me?' She sounded desperate but she didn't care. She wouldn't hide how she felt. Let him hear what he was doing to her. Let him know how this love stripped her soul bare and laid it at his feet. Let him see the precious gift he didn't believe in. But could actually have—if he would only reach out for it.

'That's all *you* can give *me*. By morning you'll belong to the grand duchy. Tonight is we all have. Take it or leave it.'

It wasn't working. Her heart lurched. Cracked. 'Leo, surely—'

'It's all that's on offer, Violetta. Take it or I walk through that door right now.'

She stared at him, confounded by what to do next. Nothing she'd said was getting through to him. His heart was seared and scored by too many wounds. How was she to reach him if not with her love? If that wasn't enough what else did she have to give?

Time.

She had that. She could be patient. If that was what it took for him to heal and be able to take the next step, she would wait. Somehow, she'd bear it. She'd dig deep and find the strength to cherish and nurture this love for the two of them.

But first she'd show him what they could have together. She'd take this night and make it unforgettable. She'd pour passion over him like a balm and make it as difficult as she could for him to just walk away.

She was staring at him. She looked shell-shocked.

Good, he needed her to understand that he couldn't do this. That loving her was not an option for him.

She'd declared her love for him but he knew he was right that her duchy would come first. Hell, the duchy had meant more to his own father than Leo, his only son, ever had. It had that pull on people. Hadn't she run away from him in the first place so she could claim it herself?

Still she said nothing.

The ravening beast in him roared in disappointment. He wanted her again but it wasn't going to happen. She was turning him down.

'So be it,' he said and started for the door.

'Leo, no,' she blurted. 'I'll take it. I'll take tonight.'

She made a little gasping sob when he reached

the door and thought she was too late and he was leaving. Then another of wild relief when he locked it and turned back and crossed the floor to her.

His own sense of relief nearly brought him to his knees.

He flung his towel away, tore the robe from her body and scooped her up, took them both down to the bed.

'Take comfort in the fact that tonight I need you,' he growled, then claimed her mouth in a savage kiss. Her hands clamped around his skull. She kissed him back. Hard. Sucked his lower lip between her teeth. Bit down. Not painful but enough to send lust surging through him.

He snatched his mouth free of hers, took her wrists and pinned them with a hand above her head. He kissed her throat, trailed his lips over her delicate collarbone, went lower to those sweet small breasts, and sucked on a distended nipple, growling in carnal satisfaction when she groaned and bucked beneath him.

Then he parted her thighs.

Desire, need, whatever the thing driving him was called, he let it take him. Wanting this scorching consummation to burn everything to the ground so by morning there'd be nothing left but dying embers and he'd be free again.

He went down on her, wrenching climax after

climax from her with his mouth. Showing her no mercy.

Or himself. Would he ever forget the taste of her?

At first, she moaned into her pillow, then dug her hands into her hair. When she was drenched in sweat, her eyes unfocused and mad with lust, he crawled back up the bed and gathered her in his arms.

Violetta shuddered as he sank into her. Enough for only the merest of the most intimate contact between them. Enough to drive them both wild. He flicked his hips again and again…waiting… waiting. Until her body jackknifed against him as a final, powerful orgasm ripped through her.

Leo buried his face in her neck and thrust into her fully, allowing himself to be lost in her for this final time. Her fractured cries, the hot wet clench of her intimate muscles around him, until there was nothing left of his grip on reality but one word. Repeated over and over.

Violetta, Violetta, Violetta…

It was a perfect summer's morning. The country that the previous forty-eight hours had devastated was bathed in glorious sunshine from a cloudless sky. But for all the damage around them you could almost imagine it had been a dream.

Luisa had arrived at seven, peeking cautiously around the door. Violetta would be grateful for ever that she'd asked no questions but just quietly got on getting her mistress ready to leave the very rooms that under different circumstances would have been hers.

What if she went to him now? Told him she'd changed her mind, that she'd marry him after all. For a brief, glorious moment Violetta imagined the world where the two of them could be together. But then she saw the von Frohburg coat of arms, fluttering high over the castle, higher than anything around them. A clear signal of who was the master here. If she went to him on his terms her duchy would be his by the law of San Nicolo, and she couldn't and wouldn't give it up, not to any man.

'The cars are here,' Luisa said. The luggage had already been taken downstairs. All there was left to do was leave herself.

Violetta walked across the room. Refusing to look again at the beautiful decor, the elegant furniture, the door to the bathroom, the vast bed, now made as if no one had slept there at all. As if she hadn't shared her last night here with the owner of this castle.

He only came to her when she stood on the castle forecourt. His car was there, at his insistence, ready to take her on the short ride to the helipad to the north of the city. Where a waiting helicopter—also his—would fly her safely back to San Nicolo.

So much care but the fact remained he was letting her go, with no further discussion about it.

He looked tired and strained as he joined her. Coming straight from a meeting with foreign dignitaries before he headed back out to help with relief efforts. For now he was dressed in an immaculate charcoal suit and grey silk tie. The antithesis of the mud-splattered jeans and shirt she'd stripped from his body last night.

He was the prince again, the monarch who'd strode into Chateau Elisabetha in full royal regalia. Not the man she'd got to know once that uniform was off. Who was she saying goodbye to? It was brutal either way, but Violetta steeled herself to it.

'I have a gift for you,' he said. 'It was tucked away in the royal collection and I thought you might like it. As a remembrance from someone you met during your stay here.'

He took her hand and placed a small velvet-covered box in her palm.

'Under other circumstances I might have felt less sanguine about you putting this in my hand.' She made a joke to hide the fact that her heart was breaking. She blinked back the moisture filling her eyes and busied herself with opening the card beneath the ribbon securing the box, but glanced up when she read it.

'From Antonio and Hildegard?'

'They didn't want you to forget them. So they

thought they'd give you something to remind you of our time together. All four of us, at the chateau.'

The corner of his mouth lifted but his eyes were filled with loss. She wanted to weep for the unfairness of it all.

Could she love this man any harder? Could he want her love any less?

'Very kind of them both when you think we never even got to meet Hildegard.'

'But she was there, somewhere. Willing us on. Hoping we would find our path in life.'

She looked into his eyes. Desperate to see something, anything, that could let her stay.

'I'm not sure we have,' she said, in a small voice.

'It's the right choice.'

'But we—'

'It's the right choice, Violetta.' He took her hands and squeezed them. 'Trust me.'

There it was again, that trust thing. But should she trust him on this?

Inside the box was an exquisite opal-and-emerald-encrusted brooch. In the shape of a spider.

'Oh, it's beautiful,' she said, gently stroking its little opal body. 'I love it. Thank you.'

Her farewells had been said. Notes of thanks written to the castle staff. The car stood waiting and there was really nothing else keeping her here. When she knew the thing she wanted above anything was denied her.

This man, and his heart.

Doomed to friendship and respect. She couldn't bear the thought of it.

She waved the little box at him. 'Tell them thank you for this.'

He gave her a tight smile and took her hand to lead her to the waiting car. Almost pushing her in. As it pulled away she couldn't stop herself from taking a last look back. Hoping he was at least watching her depart.

But he'd already turned away and was striding back to his castle, getting on with his life.

Trust him, he'd said. Perhaps in the end that was all there was left to do. Give him time and trust that somehow he'd overcome all the hurt and pain that had so ravaged his heart. And wait for him to come and claim the love she was offering.

Violetta clutched the box with her spider brooch and for now let Grimentz, and the man she loved, fall away behind her.

She turned her face to the future, to San Nicolo and all that awaited her there.

CHAPTER ELEVEN

THE PALACE CORRIDORS rang to the delighted shrieks of a toddler. A little boy being chased by a roaring lion, otherwise known as Aunt Violetta.

Maids patiently scrubbed sticky hand prints off antique furniture, footmen gathered up scattered toy animals and crouched to admire, for the umpteenth time, a beloved tractor held up for their inspection by a small, chubby fist.

But for a staff, starved for so long of the laughter of happy little ones, he was a priceless treasure who went a long way to restoring both his parents' reputations in the eyes of everyone in the palace.

Violetta had reached out to her estranged sister and invited her to visit. How could she blame her for running away from her wedding to Leo when she'd done the exact same thing?

Francesca had instantly accepted the invite. At their first meeting she'd crossed the room and gathered Violetta up in an unrestrained hug.

It felt as though she'd regained a sibling she'd never really had in the first place. She restored her sister's royal title, stripped from her when she'd eloped, and made a tiny princeling of her gorgeous little nephew. She patiently drew out her stern and taciturn brother-in-law, who had refused any honorary title of his own. He also refused to call her anything but 'Your Serene Highness' or 'ma'am', despite Violetta's efforts. She understood what had made Francesca give up everything for him.

Her sister's warrior husband was a good man.

He made no effort to curry favour or forgiveness, yet he earned it all the same as soon as anyone witnessed his behaviour around his wife and young son. His devotion melted the hardest heart.

He reminded Violetta so much of another stern, guarded man.

Having her sister back in her life was bittersweet. They'd never been close. They hadn't been allowed to—raised separately for different roles. But a new bond was developing between them and Violetta cherished it. As she did her new family.

However, it only made her longing for a family of her own more acute. And her longing for the man she wanted that family with.

Her love for Leo was a constant, as was the ache in her heart whenever she thought of him, alone, in his big, brooding fortress.

It hurt. No matter what she was doing or where she was, it hurt. Every day.

Even though on that last morning he couldn't wait to get rid of her. Opening the car door himself and just about pushing her in. He cared for her. She believed it, with every fibre of her being. He was just scared that she would let him down as his parents had.

But she recognised that too, that he'd never really been allowed to make his own choices. Oh, the irony that she was the one who'd been able to forge her own destiny. Whereas he, the powerful man, was still trapped by the expectations of his birth and the damage inflicted by his parents. She just needed to give him time to work it out for himself—that it was okay for him to choose love.

In the meantime she'd show him what true love and loyalty looked like, and she'd wait until they could meet again.

However hard he made it for her.

The people of Grimentz and San Nicolo were happily mixing in ways they hadn't for generations, but so far their respective prince and grand duchess were not.

Over the last ten months there had been several functions they were both due to attend but he'd not in the end appeared at any of them. He was busy rebuilding his country so she could understand his absence. It might have nothing to do with her being there too.

Two days ago they'd both again been on the guest list for a charity dinner. This one in Cannes. Violetta had been so filled with nervous anticipation she'd barely slept the night before. Surely he'd be there this time. She was going to see him again. Her heart had soared at the thought.

But Sebastien had arrived in his place and she couldn't pretend any more. This was the fourth event in a row where he'd failed to appear. The man was actually avoiding her.

He really had meant it when he'd said they couldn't have any kind of relationship. Short of taking a boat across Sérénité, marching up to his castle and, like the famed Elisabetha, demanding admittance, there hadn't been a way to see him again.

Except she'd been invited to the principality's May Ball and she'd hatched her crazy, daring plan. Roping in Seb to help.

She'd waited long enough. She was sure Leo loved her but obviously he wasn't prepared to do a damn thing about it. The stubborn, wonderful man would just have to be saved from himself.

And she'd have to be the one to do it.

'Everything is ready for tonight, sir.' Helene closed the leatherbound folder with her notes on the final preparations for the ball. 'The San Nicolo VIPs are arriving at eight and the grand duchess herself is due to arrive at…at…'

His head of household stammered to a stop. No doubt recalling the unspoken rule amongst his staff that no one talked about Violetta in his presence. They thought he didn't know but since she'd departed the castle that day no one had made a single mention of her and too many conversations had suspiciously halted when he'd walked into a room.

'Thank you, Helene,' he said. 'You and the team have done an excellent job.'

With a hurried curtsy and a flush of colour to her cheeks, she left.

Leo checked his watch. Four p.m. In just a few hours he would see Violetta again.

An unavoidable meeting but he was glad it was nearly here after weeks of anticipation. Good to get it over with.

He was on edge, distracted, and knew he'd get no more work done this afternoon. Irritated by his lack of discipline, he swept from the room and stalked off down the corridor with such force two Meissen figurines set by the door wobbled precariously on their consoles. He didn't much care for them aesthetically, but he kept them close by because they'd belonged to his mother. It was the one sentimentality he allowed himself about her. Perhaps the time had come to remove them, consign them to a forgotten attic.

Or, like his grand duchessa, donate them to the people.

Violetta had gifted the entire Della Torre royal art collection to the state, to sell or keep as they needed. She'd donated much of her personal wealth too, trying to swell the public purse. Then she'd embarked on a series of foreign visits to promote San Nicolo's exports and generate more trade opportunities and refill the coffers bankrupted by her uncle.

His people had loved her for it, as if she were also theirs. Loved her for everything, in fact. The press was full of her, praising every step she took with those dainty feet of hers.

As for him? He'd definitely picked up on the air of disappointment that he'd failed to make her *their* princess in reality. That there was something wanting in him that had made her turn him down.

He ignored that. What did they know? It was the other way round.

She'd declared her love for him and he'd rejected her.

Ten months since he'd virtually pushed her into that car and out of his life. Ten months since he'd turned away before she'd even left the castle forecourt and strode back into the dark maw of the castle entrance wishing it would swallow him whole.

At the time he'd told himself he'd had a lucky escape because it would inevitably have ended badly. How could their fledgling relationship have survived the rigours of running two countries facing unprecedented challenges? He told himself he was relieved.

Only the first time he walked past the empty Elisabetha suite he felt the lack of her like a gaping hole in his chest. As if all the joy had been sucked out of his world. As it had every day since. No matter how hard he tried to move on.

His anxious advisors had urged him to start searching for a new bride. Providing him with a list of eligible women. European aristocrats, poised, accomplished, perfectly qualified. Even easy on the eye.

He took the list and shoved it at the very bottom of his to-do pile.

None of them had sparked a moment's interest for him because they hadn't been her.

Leo headed towards his private gym. An hour in there might burn off the energy burning through him. It had been building ever since he'd agreed to inviting all of San Nicolo to the May Ball, which of course included their grand duchess.

His father would have berated him for being weak. Needing anyone, especially a woman, was beyond the pale for a von Frohburg prince. Yet that last night they had been together Leo had needed Violetta as much as he needed to breathe.

He'd thought he'd extinguish all that need from his body by taking her that last time. Only he hadn't. The want, the longing, had remained.

He'd convinced himself she was too young to have made her decision for life and that at some point, like his mother, she'd find something she loved more and move on.

It was as inevitable as breathing.

He'd thrown himself into work. Into the re-building of Grimentz and helping his people, barely taking a day off since the storm. It meant his country was fast recovering and his people being taken care of and it suited him to keep his days full.

It was the nights that were the problem.

Because when he was alone and tired and weak, he tortured himself by trawling the Internet for news and the latest photos.

A month before their ill-fated wedding Violetta had sat for an official portrait, in tiara and blue sash and a dress encrusted with way too many beads. She was smiling but Leo had seen the discomfort behind that demure facade and knew that someone else had chosen that outfit.

A month later came the release of her first official photograph as Grand Duchess. This time the gown was breathtakingly simple and the tiara nowhere in sight. Good girl, he thought.

Then he'd looked closer and seen what had replaced the tiara. Her up-do was decorated with a jewelled brooch, doubling as a hair ornament. Almost as valuable as any state bauble. He knew for a certainty because it had come from the Frohburg royal collection.

She'd made a modern tiara of her spider brooch.

Now each time she appeared on official duties he greedily searched for any sign that she'd used it, and sure enough each time it was there. Sitting high on a one-shouldered gown for a ballet premiere, or clipped to the ribbon waistband of a chiffon skirt on a visit to San Nicolo's state hospital, or pinned to a skull cap while braving the snow during a Memorial Day parade in wool coat and leather boots. Often it was her only embellishment and Leo knew she wore it each time to send a message to him.

I'm still here and I still love you.

No matter. One day soon she'd stop wearing it and then he'd know he'd been right to let her go.

As for her political ambitions, a nation of subjects couldn't become a democracy overnight but, by God, their new grand duchess had started her people along the route.

Announcing before her ministers had time to stop her that she was calling a referendum on making San Nicolo a democratic state. With her as their head of state...or not, whatever they decided she'd stand by.

Turned out her people loved her for it. Embracing her and her ideas. They'd voted to become a democracy and keep her and her issue as titular head of state. Even her sister had been welcomed home as the lost daughter she probably was. Bringing a small son with her, who had the brown eyes of the Della Torres and the black hair of his English father.

A son that looked like him and Violetta. When

he'd seen that picture it had taken Leo several minutes to be able to breathe normally again.

Of their own accord Leo's feet took him to the Elisabetha suite. As they often had since that one night when Violetta was there.

The rooms were immaculate, of course, but they felt fresh and vivid, alive somehow. As if their owner had just stepped out and left a vital shimmer of energy behind her.

What owner? Grimentz was without a crown princess. He had no mate to inhabit these rooms and fill them with a feminine warmth and welcome. They'd been no oasis when his mother had been in possession of them but that single night, when Violetta had been mistress here, he'd found solace.

And passion like he'd never known.

From the window, his gaze was drawn across the waters of Lake Sérénité to San Nicolo, sunning itself on this perfect May afternoon. The duchy palace itself wasn't quite visible from here, tucked away in a curve of the lake shore, but he could see Violetta's standard fluttering over the city rooftops and knew she was in residence. It would be a place of welcome, he knew, despite all the difficulties her duchy faced.

He might not have been able to have her in his life but he'd wanted so badly to help her and he did what he could.

That first week he'd had his own head of security recommend a good man to her ministers. To-masz, once formally hired, had gathered a strong team around his new employer and Leo had felt some relief knowing she was at least well protected.

The research he'd ordered on her prime minister proved what he'd already believed from the conversation they'd had. She had a capable, honest and loyal man advising her.

He'd have poured money into her little, broke state but even concealing company behind company it would only take one determined journalist to uncover the truth, as inevitably someone would, and Leo would be accused of trying to annexe the duchy by stealth.

Instead he'd contacted everyone with wealth and influence that he knew. Charming, cajoling, or bluntly calling in favours so that she'd get the assistance she needed. Offers of help began landing on the desk of her finance minister. For who'd dare risk alienating the powerful Prince of Grimentz by refusing?

There was nothing official to be done about her uncle. The man had made poor choices, not illegal ones. For a time he'd caused as much fuss as possible. He'd released his autobiography filled with 'secrets' that had painted the Della Torres as grasping imbeciles and his youngest niece the worst of all, causing a storm across the world.

But she'd weathered it. His brave, beautiful

girl had weathered it all. Her people had closed ranks around her, lent her their strength, and she'd emerged stronger and more popular still.

Her uncle, however, had found suddenly that he was no longer welcome in any of the grand houses of Europe. In the States his lucrative second book deal had been cancelled and across the world invites for interviews and TV appearances had gradually dried up. There didn't seem to be any connection. Who had that wide an influence?

One man perhaps. You made an enemy of the Prince of Grimentz—or hurt something he cared about—and you'd come to regret it.

The two countries had retained the new kinship that had emerged from the storm. Some that had come to help with the rescue efforts had stayed. Others invited to take temporary refuge in San Nicolo had decided not to return. There'd been numerous marriages and many babies now on the way.

Children.

He'd never imagined he'd feel the profound lack of a child in his life. Not just because he needed an heir, but because he wanted to be a father.

Leo closed his eyes, blocking out the view of San Nicolo.

No, that wasn't accurate.

He didn't just want to be a father. He wanted to be the father of Violetta's children.

But of course that couldn't happen. He wanted

to have respect and admiration for his future princess but how Violetta made him feel was so much more than that. It gave her the power to hurt him and he wouldn't let anyone hurt him again.

The May Ball was tonight. This year, not only was every citizen of Grimentz invited to the city for the festivities as usual, but, by way of a thank you for all their assistance since the storm, everyone from San Nicolo was also invited.

Their grand duchess, too.

They would finally meet again in person. It was time to let go of this infatuation. The May Ball would be the perfect opportunity for that. He might even discover she no longer held the fascination for him that she had.

He turned his back on the suite and its glorious view to Violetta's standard sailing proudly in the spring breeze. Closed the door softly and vowed he wouldn't cross the threshold again until his new princess was found and installed there.

It was well past time to move on.

CHAPTER TWELVE

LEO HAD TRIED on three tuxedos and rejected them all. Even his perfectionist valet was at a loss to the objections.

Something wrong with the fit. Shoulders weren't sitting right. Not black enough, too black.

'Too black?' Matteo asked, looking at him as if he'd lost it. 'May I remind sir, it's a *black tie* event?'

'I look too austere, too unapproachable. What about my white dinner jacket?'

His valet's lips pursed in distaste.

'Sir, if you insist on wearing the white dinner jacket this evening, then expect to find my letter of resignation on your desk in the morning. I would have no other choice.'

'What sartorial faux pas has he threatened this time?' said Seb, strolling in.

Dressed in an immaculate white dinner jacket.

Leo made a face and threw up his hands.

'Yes, well, if His Serene Highness will insist on looking like a pirate...' Matteo's lip curled as

he studied Leo's overlong hair and new beard '...
he must accept his choices for evening wear will
be limited.'

Leo suppressed a sigh. 'I just want to look right
this evening.'

'In what way were the three perfectly appropriate tuxedos not accomplishing that?' his valet
asked in exasperation.

Hell, Leo thought, *I am losing it.*

He'd see her. He'd smile. He'd exchange pleas-
antries. They'd share a dance, as would be expected of them, then he'd move on to his other
guests.

He made his decision. She couldn't be in his
life and he'd live with it.

Seb was helping himself to a brandy. 'I came by
before I go to collect my date because I thought
you'd like an update on the charity dinner.'

The one held two days ago, that Leo had been
invited to but had at the last minute conjured up
something or other that had absolutely required
his personal attendance—as he had for every
function he and Violetta had both been due to attend—and for this one sent Seb in his place.

'Thanks. No update needed.'

Seb's glass paused on the way to his lips.

'You're not going to ask how she was? Or what
I discovered?'

He yearned to know.

'It's not really of interest,' he said, casually collecting a cufflink from its box. 'But as you're apparently burning to tell me, what did you discover?'

'She's working very long hours, she's losing weight, and that she seems rather attached to a certain opal and emerald spider brooch that bears a remarkable resemblance to one I remember seeing in the vaults here.'

Leo fumbled the metal bar he was sliding through his cuff.

She'd lost weight. His petite Violetta was already tiny enough.

He willed his fingers to be steady.

'I see. And you think this concerns me how?'

'Well, I was just curious who gave her that brooch and whether that same person may still be concerned for her welfare.'

Leo willed his fingers to be steady and threaded the cufflink.

Who was looking after her, making sure she ate well, got sufficient sleep? Luisa appeared competent, and obviously cared about her mistress, but Violetta was stubborn. Would she listen, do as she was told, eat properly, rest? Goddamn it, he hated being so helpless to do anything.

'You broke her heart, you know,' Seb said.

Matteo paused in brushing the tuxedos, listening intently.

Leo frowned to mask the sudden crushing pain in his chest.

'She wanted something I wasn't able to give. I did her a kindness. It would have ended badly.'

'So two people, who are meant to be together, living alone and miserable is a good ending?'

'I didn't know you could be so sentimental,' Leo drawled.

'You're in love with her. Everyone knows it, except you!' He scrutinised Leo's face. 'Or you do, which makes what you did to her even worse.'

Seb marched over to inspect one of the rejected tuxedos.

'Matteo, he'll wear this midnight-blue Armani, with the shawl lapel. Perfect for the evening's festivities, wouldn't you agree?'

'My thoughts exactly,' Matteo said, holding up the jacket for Leo to slip into. 'Come along now, sir, chop-chop. You heard Prince Sebastien. We wouldn't want you to be late for your own party.'

Leo snatched the jacket from his valet's hands and shrugged into it. 'Since when did you two become so managing?'

'Since you decided to invite the whole of San Nicolo and its grand duchess to the ball,' Seb said. 'And you've barely been able to string two sentences together.'

'That's not true. I've been… I've had… There's been lots of…'

Sebastien laughed, knocked back his brandy, dumped the empty tumbler and headed towards the door. 'Matteo, I'll leave him in your care. I'm off to collect Violetta from her hotel. Let's hope she isn't having the same trouble deciding what to wear or this party might go ahead without any of us in attendance.'

Leo looked up.

'Violetta?'

'Didn't I mention it? She asked me to be her escort for the evening. You don't mind, do you?'

The thought of it slammed into his gut like a clenched fist. Was Violetta developing feelings for his cousin? Because the man was no more available to her than Leo himself. Seb's heart was already spoken for. Not that he'd admit to it—like Leo, he had his demons—but there would only ever be one woman for Seb and Violetta wasn't her.

Was she about to get hurt all over again? Seb wouldn't pursue her, Leo knew that. But had she given up waiting and set her hopes on his cousin?

He wouldn't let that happen. Because... Because...

It was just that he didn't want her to hurt any more, not if he could help it. That was all. He didn't...he couldn't...*love* her.

As the lamplight caught in the emeralds, Violetta's precious brooch sparkled in her fingers. She was nearly ready. All that was needed was for Luisa to fix it into her hair.

Her gown was a simple, ivory silk sheath, with

shoestring straps and diaphanous chiffon layers. She adored the way it floated round her as she moved. It felt so romantic.

Perfect for the evening.

If her plans worked. The ones she'd cooked up with Seb at that gala dinner.

Her stomach lurched. What if Leo still couldn't choose happiness?

Wearing his brooch had never held such significance as tonight. Her fingers trembled as she gazed down on it.

The gift she'd treasured from the moment Leo had placed it in her hands. No one knew it came from the von Frohburg royal collection. When asked she'd simply said that it was a gift and she'd fallen in love with it.

Not with the gift giver, of course.

Violetta stroked the opal body of her beloved little spider. She knew the precise moment Leo had stolen her heart. When he'd made up that story about Antonio the spider to ease her fears.

And the moment he'd broken it? When he'd placed this brooch in her hand then turned and walked away as if he'd forgotten her already.

Seb had said he hadn't, that he was miserable without her.

Of all the challenges she'd faced in the last ten months this was the hardest. Seeing Leo again, speaking to him, taking his hand…and then all those other things she hoped for.

The knock on the door heralded Seb's arrival. Still clutching the brooch in her fingers, she entered the sitting room where he waited.

His gaze swept her from head to toe. 'Why, Grand Duchessa, you are a vision.'

She blushed a little beneath his scrutiny. 'Thank you. You look very handsome yourself.'

'Oh, I'm just the poor cousin. I leave the real glamour to Leo. He does stern and majestic aloofness so well.' He bent to kiss her cheek.

'How is he?' she asked.

'Demanding, irritable, pompous. You know, his usual charming self.'

That won him a nervous smile.

Then his brow creased. 'But where is it?'

Violetta opened her palm to reveal the brooch. 'You mean this?' She tilted her hand so the light caught in the milky opal at its centre. 'What if my plan doesn't work, Sebastien? What if I can't change his mind?'

He placed a knuckle beneath her chin. 'Well, then, the Grand Duchess of San Nicolo will hold her head up high, in this ravishing wisp of a gown and her extraordinary signature piece, and leave every other overdressed creature at the party gnashing their teeth with envy.'

'You know how to make a girl feel better.'

He grinned and waited while Luisa fixed the brooch into the unstructured bun that sat low at the back of her head.

'Perfect,' he said and held out his arm. 'Ready?'

Violetta placed her hand in the crook of his elbow, suddenly grateful to have this tall, charming man to lean on.

'As I'll ever be.' She straightened her spine. 'Okay, let's go get him.'

The peoples of Grimentz and San Nicolo had gathered in their thousands.

The principality laying on the mother of all parties to thank their neighbours. Those neighbours gladly accepting; in their entirety, judging by the crowds.

There were hog roasts in every city square with live music and dancing in every street. For the dignitaries, and the ordinary citizens honoured with special invites, the terraced gardens of the castle had been transformed into a fairyland, with thousands of tiny lights draped over every pergola, above every path, through every tree. Even the brooding fortress looming overhead had a touch of frivolity to it, with its own light show of ever-changing colours. Projected onto the very centre of the ancient ramparts were the flags of Grimentz and San Nicolo fluttering proudly together for all the world to see.

Below on the lake it looked as though every boat that either country possessed had also been pressed into service. Sérénité was filled with them. Some lashed together side by side, with partygoers mixing freely via the gangways running across the decks between them, or smaller boats coming alongside, handing up baskets laden with pastries and cheese and bottles of wine.

The sounds floated up to where Violetta was walking with Seb towards the party. The chatter of happy conversation, the flurry of groans and laughter as a basket lurched and half its contents landed in the lake.

She could see platters being passed from boat to boat. Wine from Grimentz, baskets of bread and pastries. The reverse of what had happened after the storm, Grimentz intent on saying thank you to its neighbour. San Nicolo determined that the new accord should continue.

Helene appeared through the guests, her smile of welcome genuine. As had everyone's been since Violetta had arrived in the city earlier that afternoon and taken her suite in the hotel.

'Helene, you and your team are to be congratulated,' Violetta said. 'It all looks wonderful.'

'His Highness had high expectations for this one. It's come together, of course, but it has been a challenge.'

'I'm sure he's been very complimentary.'

'I wouldn't bet on it,' Seb murmured.

Helene sent him a rueful smile as Matteo arrived beside them.

'Your Highness,' he said with a bow, 'permit me to say you are utter perfection this evening.'

'Thank you, Matteo. From you that's high praise indeed.'

'Everything you requested is in place, ma'am,' Helene said. 'We're ready to go the moment you say the word.'

Violetta shot a quick glance to the party but couldn't see Leo yet.

'We'll have to see if he agrees first,' she said.

'If he does not, I'm resigning forthwith,' Matteo said.

'You'd do no such thing.' Violetta laughed. 'You love him and wouldn't leave him.'

'Isn't that just the tragedy of it?' Matteo sighed. 'The dratted man makes it so hard to love him and yet somehow we all do.'

'Speak for yourself,' Seb said. 'These last ten months have severely tested my patience.'

'Today every single member of castle staff has received a gift and a handwritten card with a personal message of thanks for all their efforts since the storm,' Helene said. 'Ma'am, myself and the handful of castle staff who've been involved with your requests are rooting for you. We hope your plan works. The prince deserves to be happy and that's not how he's been since you left.'

Would she succeed in that? Violetta thought, with a twist to her stomach as she heard Leo's voice up ahead, greeting other new arrivals. The elderly guest he'd been greeting moved off and now Violetta could see him.

She drank in the sight. His height, his broad shoulders. Those eyes that could make you feel like the only creature in the world. The beautifully cut tuxedo that showed off his impressive physique. He looked leaner, darker. More forbidding even than she remembered, and his lustrous hair was longer. It curled over his collar. He'd even grown a beard. All in all, it was only just on the right side of untamed.

Heaven help her, it was… Oh, God, it was *hot*.

Her throat tightened. Her mouth went dry. What if she tried to greet him and nothing came out?

'Your Highness…' Seb was saying.

She tried to catch her breath. Was she hyper-ventilating? Here, amongst all these people, with nowhere to run and hide. She was. She actually couldn't breathe.

Then Leo looked up. Their eyes met.

'Grand Duchessa?' Seb's voice came again.

What if she fainted? Right here. Oh, how mor-tifying—

'Violetta!'

She jumped, looking up to see Seb grimacing.

'If it's all the same to you I'd like to retain the use of my arm after tonight.'

He sent a pained look to where her fingers were clenched in a death grip on his sleeve.

'I'm so sorry. It's just—'

'I know. But relax!' Seb whispered as Leo began walking towards them. 'Trust me, it's all going to be fine.'

But what if it wasn't?

CHAPTER THIRTEEN

Leo had known the instant she'd joined the guests mingling on the terrace. Glimpsing the slight figure in floating ivory through the crowd on the arm of his cousin.

The aged princess, whose gnarled fingers he'd just taken, winced as his hand convulsed around hers. He made his apologies as she moved off.

His attention slewed straight back to Violetta. She was even more beautiful than he remembered. Her rich brown hair caught up in an unstructured knot. Her dress, a simple gossamer sheath. On any other it would have been a shapeless sack, but of her it made a goddess. Ethereal, and gorgeous. He wanted to gaze at her for ever. He wanted to fall on his knees and worship at her feet.

Leo knew he'd badly misjudged. That even seeing her with Seb was going to be too much; his cousin, who his calm, rational head knew for a certainty would never *ever* betray him. But all that mattered to the slavering, jealous beast that reared up inside him was that Seb was another male and he was standing too close to her.

For one crazed moment he actually thought about turning on his heel and just walking out of there. Quitting the party where he was host. But then he spied Helene, talking to Violetta, and whatever vestige of reason was clinging on reminded him of all the work that she and the castle team had done to put this evening together, and he knew he couldn't do it, couldn't let any of his people down by taking the coward's way out and leaving.

Instead he headed straight towards her. Aiming to get their meeting out of the way. The blood was rushing in his ears. Despite the pleasant breeze coming off the lake a trickle of sweat slid down his back.

Then there she stood.

He devoured the sight as a starved man hungered after a banquet. The sweetly pointed chin, those warm eyes, and slender limbs.

'Good evening, Your Serene Highness.'

'Good evening, Grand Duchessa.' Leo took the proffered hand and bowed over it. He made a little heel click. 'Thank you for being so gracious as to join us this evening. I trust you are well?' His voice would barely work. Could he sound any more stilted?

'Oh, yes, thank you. I'm… I'm very well.'

Violetta's glance flickered to Seb in bewilderment. When she looked back to Leo, Seb mouthed at him.

'Stop being a dick.'

To his right Leo heard Matteo make a frustrated groan.

He tried to pull himself together, to be the charming host, but while her hand sat in the crook of his cousin's elbow it was liking asking a starving wolf to sit calmly, and be petted, while a tender lamb stood nearby.

The orchestra stirred to life.

'Do you mind?' he said, not waiting for Seb's answer but taking Violetta's hand and transferring it to his arm instead.

'The dancing is about to begin and the grand duchess and I should set the example.'

He might as well have been on a tumbril, being dragged through the crowd to his execution, not walking amongst his invited guests, the man beside her looked so grim and dark.

They reached the centre of the dance floor set up on the largest of the terraces. With only the briefest glance at her, Leo took her in hold.

She remembered the last time he'd held her like this. She'd been wearing nothing but ballet shoes and his shirt, and he hadn't been able to keep his gaze—or his hands—off her. Now it was as if he could barely stand to touch her at all.

'You clearly aren't taking proper care of your-

self,' he said as the music began. 'Do you even ob-
serve mealtimes? You're practically skin and bone.'

Perhaps she'd lost a kilo or two. She might not
have eaten at regular times, she often worked late
into the night, there'd been so much to do, but
Luisa always made sure she ate something.

'Thank you for the gracious compliment,' she
said as they danced past other couples joining
them on the floor, couples who were trying val-
iantly not to stare.

His lip curled. 'It's merely an observation from
one monarch to another. You'll be no use to your
duchy if you aren't fit enough to work.'

'I'm fortunate that not all the von Frohburgs
have forgotten their manners this evening. Prince
Sebastien was much more of a gentleman.'

That earned her a swift glare. 'A word of advice, Violetta. If you are setting your sights on my
cousin you should know he won't be interested.'

Her brow creased. 'What?'

'You asked him to be your date for the evening. I assumed that you might be developing a
tendre for him.'

Fury lit up inside her. How dared he? How
could he?

Here she was being all misty-eyed about how
alone he was, how much he must be missing her.
Yet what did he do when they finally met again?
Insult her, then patronise her and then accuse her,
casually, of crushing on someone else. When she'd

been breaking her heart every moment of the last ten months waiting for him to wake up and come and claim her love at last.

'I don't care for what you're implying.'

'I was trying to be helpful.'

'By insulting me?'

He tightened his grip on her waist as he navigated a brief congestion on the dance floor.

'By advising you.'

'I already have enough advisors.'

'In this case they would say the same, trust me.'

'There it is again. That trust thing that you're so big on. But trusting you hasn't served me that well before.'

'Take it or leave it. I'm just advising you to choose someone else instead.'

'Who, Leo? Which paragon of masculinity do you have in mind?'

He scowled as his cousin swirled past them with a voluptuous brunette in his arms. 'I don't know, someone...*else*.'

She rolled her eyes and just in case he hadn't got the message, gave an exasperated sigh too.

'It can't be me, if that's what you're angling for.'

She snatched her hand from his and stopped dead.

'Angling?' Numerous heads swivelled in their direction, but she didn't care who heard. She was too angry. Too hurt. Was he really saying these callous things to her? 'You make it sound like you're the prize. Well, I've got news for you, you're not. I am, and I'll bestow myself wherever the hell I choose.'

'Who here doesn't know that you're the prize?' Leo said, flinging out a protective arm as another couple threatened to dance straight into her. 'Which creature watching your rise over the last few months hasn't worked out you're the most extraordinary human being ever to come out of San Nicolo, or Grimentz for that matter?'

'*You*, apparently, because if you had you would have never let me go.'

She spun away from him and began weaving her way through the other dancers.

'Where are you going?' he demanded.

'Anywhere that's away from you.' The Arctic Circle. No, the Antarctic. That was further.

'I haven't finished yet.'

'Trust me. You have nothing left to say that I want to hear.'

She reached the edge of the dance floor and stepped down onto the path. The goggling crowds parted as the Grand Duchess of San Nicolo stormed past with the Prince of Grimentz in hot pursuit.

Violetta spied an arbour, tucked away in a quiet corner of the garden. Desperate to get away from Leo, from everyone, from this whole miserable evening, she hitched up her hem and ran towards it. She groaned in frustration when she discovered it was already occupied.

With those long legs of his Leo easily matched her stride.

'You will excuse us,' Leo ordered and with no attempt at politeness. He looked so fierce Violetta suspected an entire platoon of his guardsmen would have thought twice before remaining where they were.

As it was, an actual guardsman from Grimentz and a San Nicolo doctor—Violetta recognised her from a recent visit to the state hospital—swiftly unwound from their passionate clinch and shot to their feet. With a bow for Leo and a curtsy for her, they beat their retreat.

'Isn't it obvious I don't want to talk to you?'

He folded his arms across his chest. 'I need you to know that Seb's not the man for you.'

She flung up her hands. 'I have no interest in Sebastien. Even though he is infinitely more charming. Much less frustrating, pig-headed, overbearing, patronising, pompous.'

Leo's brow rose. 'Now who's dishing out insults?'

'You deserve every one of them.'

She sat down. The layers of her dress settling around her with an indignant sigh. 'I had such high hopes for this evening.'

'I hoped merely to get through it.'

She looked up at him with a frown. 'What do you mean?'

He glowered at a terracotta pot of pretty tumbling geraniums but remained stubbornly silent.

'You broke my heart, you know.'

'So I've been told.'

'Don't you even care that you hurt me?'

'It had to be done.'

'Why, Leo? Why was it so damn necessary to rip my heart to shreds?'

'I would have hurt you eventually anyway, because I can't give you want you want.'

'And what is that? What is it you think I want that you can't give me?'

'You know the answer to that already.' He shot a look at her over his shoulder. 'Love,' he said.

'Leo, you already behave like a man in love. I know you've been using your influence to help me.'

He waved a dismissive hand. 'I'd have done the same for any neighbouring monarch in difficulties.'

'Including going to great lengths to make a social pariah of her uncle so he couldn't embarrass her further?'

His jaw tightened, and his mouth compressed into a determined line of silence.

She studied him sadly. 'Thank you for that. It helped me a lot at the time.'

He half turned towards her as if drinking in that nugget of information. But then he looked straight ahead.

'It doesn't matter anyway. Love does not work well in royal marriages.'

'Nonsense. There are numerous examples where it's thrived.'

'Very well, I'll amend that. Love would not belong in *my* marriage.'

'And why is that?'

'It's not something I want.'

'That's only because you're scared.'

He kept a determined silence.

'Admit it, Leo. You're frightened.'

His jaw tightened…again.

'I'll live with it,' he said. 'It doesn't change anything.'

Oh. *Oh.*

Finally she might be getting somewhere. He'd erred, he'd revealed a tiny weakness in his hard shell of supposed indifference. He knew it too. He straightened himself, his posture even more tense.

'And how's that working for you? Being alone up there in your big old fortress? I've heard you're miserable. That you haven't been the same since I left.'

He folded his arms across his chest and transferred his glare to an entirely innocent bed of rosemary. 'You shouldn't believe everything you hear.'

'You're going to deny it? You're going to deny that you miss me?'

'I've been extremely busy.'

'How is that an answer?' She moved in front of him. Blocking his way out of the arbour. He'd have to pick her up to get past her, to touch her, and she had the sense that if he did, he wouldn't be able to stop. 'Well, that's not good enough for me any more.'

'You have no choice.'

'No? Perhaps not, but you know me. I'm big on finding alternative solutions to a problem. I'm taking charge here and I'm going to paint a picture for you, so you can truly understand the consequences of the choice you're making.'

She lifted her chin to stare right at him.

'You let me go now and this is what will happen. I want children. Your children, specifically.'

His eyes glittered.

'But if you won't do the job then I'll have to find someone who will, and I'll do it. For San Nicolo. I'm still Head of State and my people need an heir.'

He stared down his nose at her, but his eyes flashed.

'That means there'll have to be a man in my life. Allowed to put his hands on me. Imagine that for a moment, Leo. Seb just took my arm in platonic friendship and I know you couldn't handle it. You looked positively murderous back there.'

That muscle in his jaw was working overtime. 'You can even see my standard from your castle. You'll know when I'm home, with my husband, and what we'll be doing in bed together, night after night.' She pushed her face into his. 'Until I'm pregnant.'

'Violetta,' he warned. 'Stop this.'

'He'll hold me, kiss me, touch every intimate inch of me. You know how I like to be touched, don't you, Leo?' she purred.

He was utterly still, rigid but for the tic of a muscle in his jaw.

'So let me ask you. What frightens you more? How you feel now or how you'd feel then?'

'Violetta.' It was part anger, part desperation and wrenched from the depths of him as if he'd been gutted and left to bleed.

'Bothers you, doesn't it? That image.'

She reached up to stroke a lapel. His big frame shuddered beneath her touch. As if she'd run her fingers over naked skin, not finely tailored satin.

She was getting to him and she wouldn't spare him a single detail. She'd make him admit how he felt. She was done with letting him hide away.

'And when there's a baby, Leo, an heir, a little boy or girl. What will you feel then?'

'Violetta.' His voice dropped to the barest whisper. 'Please stop.'

'No, Leo. I won't. Not until you give me a damn good reason why we can't be together. We so obviously love each other, and don't even bother trying to deny it.'

He couldn't help himself. He reached out to lightly touch the brooch in her hair.

'You wear this all the time.'

Eyes dark and compelling as midnight gazed up at him, filled with all the emotions he was trying so hard to suppress in himself. 'You must know why?'

He let out a long, slow, shuddering breath. 'You're trying to tell me you still love me.'

'Yes.' So sure, so utterly certain. How he envied her that.

'But what if we can't make it work? What if our duties get in the way?'

'Leo, I've just saved my country from financial ruin. You've just rebuilt yours after Mother Nature did her worst. Compared to all that, co-ordinating two schedules will be a breeze.'

She made it sound so simple. But there was more to this than that.

'What if I can't make you happy? What if I'm too broken to love you back?' It was a dark confession.

'Are you?' Her hands settled flat against his jacket and the comfort of a honeyed warmth spread through him. 'You feel pretty whole to me.'

She placed an ear to his chest. She'd easily hear his heartbeat. It was pounding so hard anyone within ten metres would be able to hear it.

'Yup, all sounds fine and dandy. Nothing broken in there.'

'I drove my mother away because I didn't love her enough. It was my fault she left.' He could hear Leo the boy in that statement, but it was time for honesty and there was, after all this time, a part of him that believed it.

Fierce now, Violetta reached up to take his face in her hands. 'Firstly, your mother didn't want love. She wanted adulation. Secondly, she didn't leave because of you, she left because of your father, but he was too much of a coward to admit it so he pretended it was your fault.'

'Neither of them loved me. I'm not someone that people love, Violetta.'

There.

He'd finally said it. The truth he'd buried deep, but had carried with him for years, rooted like a malign growth in his soul. 'You think you care for me now but…' his voice cracked '…you'll change your mind.'

She gently scuffed her knuckles back and forth along his bearded jaw. 'Oh, my darling man, you really won't get rid of me that easily. I love you. I'll always love you. Believe it. Despite your efforts to keep everyone at arm's length. Seb, Matteo, your people, while she was with us, your wonderful *grand-mère*. We all love you—we can't help ourselves. You're a good man.'

Leo's throat closed.

Above their heads the image of their respective flags fluttered together on his castle walls. On the garden paths and the dance floor, Grimentzians and San Nicoloans were together.

Why could he not do the same? Why could he not reach out for happiness, for love?

Because of a woman who failed her only child? A father who was so cold-hearted all he could teach his son was to gaze with avarice at his neighbours?

But Leo wasn't either of them. He served his people well. He'd been like a brother to Seb. He'd let go of the need to grasp San Nicolo because it was morally right. He'd supported its grand duchess in every way he could and here she stood, offering him her heart.

Violetta had risen above all the limitations her family had placed on her life and surpassed them all. Leading her people into a bright, new future.

How could he think of letting such a woman slip through his fingers just because he was afraid?

How could he leave the way open for another man…?

A possessive rage reared up inside him.

He would *not*.

He gathered her up and crushed her to him.

'No other man will be the father of your children, Violetta,' he growled. She was so slight in his arms and yet she felt like his anchor, like a safe harbour in the storm. He dropped to the bench and drew her onto his lap. He dropped his forehead against hers. 'You're right. My life is nothing without you because I love you, too. Marry me. *Save* me.'

She let out a long sigh of contentment and wound her arms about his neck. 'Yes, Leo,' she said, 'I will.' Her fingers toyed with the hair that curled over his collar. A shadow fell briefly over her eyes. 'You've scolded me for not taking care of myself, but you've also worked too hard and I know why,' she said, sadly. 'You focused on fixing your country so you wouldn't have to think about fixing yourself. That stops now. We can fix you together. A day at a time. Here, or in San Nicolo. Or both. Commuting would be easy and I'd rather like riding in that fancy helicopter of yours.'

'I don't care where I live as long as it's with you,' he said and stopped any further discussion by sealing their bargain with a kiss.

When they strolled back onto the path hand in hand, Seb was waiting for them. Helene and Matteo hovered a few paces behind.

'Well?' Seb asked, glancing down at their entwined hands.

Violetta stared up at Leo with a glorious smile. 'Yes.'

'Finally. I thought I might have to start a fight so I could beat some sense into you.'

'We're a go then, ma'am?' Helene asked.

'We're a go.'

'I'll get the chef to bring out the cake.'

'The luggage is ready, Your Highness.' Matteo popped up behind Seb. 'I'll have it taken down to

the castle forecourt.' With a swift bow he spun on
his heel and followed Helene.

Leo frowned. 'Cake? Luggage? What's going on?'

Violetta took both his hands and smiled up at
him. 'I thought we could get married.'

'What? *Now?*'

'Yes, now! Our people are here to bear witness.
As is your archbishop. And he conveniently has all
the documentation we would have used last July.
It's all still legal. I checked with him.'

Leo's eyes narrowed on her. 'You planned all
this?'

She studied him from beneath her lashes. 'You
don't mind, do you?'

No, he thought, not even a little bit. He didn't
want to waste another moment of his life without her.

For answer he gathered her up and kissed her.
'If we're going to do this, there's something I need
to collect from the palace first.' He was about to
stride away but turned back suddenly and caught
up her hands. 'You will be here when I get back,
won't you?'

Violetta's face lit up in a smile that made him
giddy as a schoolboy.

'Yes, I'll be here,' she said. 'I'll always be here
for you, Leo.'

Guests had squeezed into every available spot
around the dance floor. Royalty and subjects alike,

jostling for the best view. Leo's castle staff filled the battlements or craned for a better view on the walkways, some were even tucked in cheek by jowl amongst the VIP guests.

He paced nervously at the edge of the dance floor. Behind him, beneath a flower-strewn arch placed there by four footmen under the careful direction of Helene, the archbishop waited to perform the marriage ceremony.

Then his bride appeared.

Leo's heart just about stopped as she walked towards him, all light and joy and spellbinding loveliness. She carried a bouquet of roses his gardeners had gathered for her. A gardenia was tucked behind her ear.

But her dazzling smile was all her own and all for him.

She reached the edge of the dance floor and placed her hand in his. His nerves fled; his heart swelled. He knew for certain that nothing he'd done in his life had ever been so right.

The ceremony was broadcast across both countries, on the giant screens in the squares, onto the castle ramparts. All the people of San Nicolo and Grimentz were able to bear witness to this union.

When the archbishop asked Violetta, 'Do you take this man?' her yes was answered by a great roar that went up across the city and through the flotilla gathered below.

Before Leo could answer his own question one of his footmen shouted, 'Don't do it, sir.'

A nearby butler gave him a good-natured cuff for his pains, but laughter rippled through the guests. Violetta was helpless with giggles, her smile growing even wider.

Leo raised their clasped hands to his lips. 'I do,' he said, and this time the roar of voices was accompanied by car horns blasting across the city and then sirens, as the boats gathered on the lake joined in.

The archbishop was obliged to wait several minutes before he could continue. He beckoned to the best man. Seb stepped up and opened his palm. Where two gold bands sat. The rings that had been ordered for the wedding last year.

When Violetta looked up in surprise, Leo gave her a crooked smile.

'I kept them. For some reason I couldn't bring myself to let them go.'

After he'd placed the plain gold band on her finger, he retrieved a second ring from his pocket and slipped that too on her finger.

'Your engagement ring,' he said. Running his thumb over the exquisite rectangular-cut emerald set with a diamond on each compass point.

When they were pronounced husband and wife, the great cacophony erupted up again, joined by fireworks.

But Leo barely heard any of it. He was too busy sealing his marriage with a kiss for his bride.

There was a toast, in the finest champagne, and the cutting of a cake. Leo marvelled at the towering masterpiece his kitchen team had created. Five tiers that bore the Grimentzian and San Nicolo coats of arms wound together in royal icing. The Grimentzian guardsman from earlier, with a wry grin, presented his sword to the colonel-in-chief and his new bride so they might perform the ceremonial cut into the bottom layer.

Then came their first dance.

A waltz, of course.

Specifically the one they'd danced to at the chateau.

When his bride looked at him in surprise, Leo sent her his best angelic smile.

'I thought you'd appreciate something familiar as you're dancing in public.' He drew her close, pressed his mouth to her ear. 'I have you safe, *il mio diletto principessa*, so set free your dancing heart.'

In his arms, happier than she could ever express, his beloved princess did...

On the castle forecourt, decked out with streamers and a handwritten 'Just Married' sign, waited a red Ferrari. Seb stood beside it, the keys dangling from his fingers.

'Please don't drive it into a ditch this time,' he said.

Leo took the keys with a glare. 'It was not a ditch. It was an unavoidable pothole.'

'Don't worry, Seb,' Violetta said, climbing into the passenger seat. 'I'm with him now. I'll make sure your Ferrari is safe.'

Leo drove them out of the city. Their security following at a discreet distance.

'I have a surprise of my own,' he said. 'I did what you suggested. I've reopened Chateau Elisabetha. I haven't been there much yet, but I thought we could start our honeymoon there.'

The roads had been repaired, any storm damage cleared away and the track up to the house re-Tarmacked. Seb's car was spared any misfortunes.

As they passed the treeline and saw the chateau in all its glory, Violetta gasped. The steps up to the front door were lined with storm lanterns, filled with candles. Inside the stairs were similarly lined, candles lighting their way upstairs to the master suite. Where a bottle of champagne on ice awaited them.

'Oh, Leo. It's absolutely perfect. Who knew you were an old romantic under that gruff exterior?'

'Only with you,' he said, backing her towards the bed and finding the zip on her dress at the same time.

Later, as Violetta slept in his arms—making contented little snuffling noises that utterly delighted him—Leo scrolled through pictures already circulating from the wedding. One in particular caught his attention.

They were standing on a terrace edge, acknowledging the crowds gathered below. His hand was flung high in an unrestrained wave, the other was wrapped around Violetta's waist. He was looking at the crowd below, but she was gazing up at him. And the expression in her eyes?

It was complete devotion.

Love.

Leo's hand came up to his mouth.

'What is it? What's wrong?'

Violetta had stirred in his arms.

'Nothing.' He pressed his lips to her brow. 'It's nothing.'

'Oh, no. We're not doing that.' She reached over him to throw on the bedside light. 'Tell me.'

She was studying him anxiously, but he took her left hand and held it up so he could admire the emerald ring on her finger. 'So, you like this, then?'

'You're changing the subject.'

He let out a shaky breath. 'Humour me? Just for a moment. Please.'

Her face softened. 'Okay. Yes, of course. I love it.'

'I knew you would. You have such a fondness for emeralds.'

She rolled her eyes at him.

'This one comes from the same collection your tiara did.'

'It was inspired by the plucky Elisabetha?'

'Yes, but I didn't tell you her whole story.'

She lifted up to look into his face. 'You're not about to tell me she sacrificed herself and died a horrible death, are you? Because that's not the kind of story a bride wants to hear on her wedding night.'

'No.' His hand cupped the back of her head and drew her closer for a kiss. 'Nothing like that.' He waited until she'd settled her chin propped on his hand, which lay on his chest. 'She didn't just save Grimentz through moral duty. She gave herself to the prince for love.'

Violetta's eyes grew wide. 'For love? I like her even more now.'

'Thought you might. The story goes that they met at her father's court months before the siege, and though he was guarded and gruff she saw through that, to the man he was beneath his wounds. Beyond his pain.' Leo's hand slid to cup Violetta's cheek. 'She fell in love with him. That's why she married him, not just to save Grimentz, but because she wanted to spend her life with him.'

He paused but Violetta waited patiently. Giving him the time he needed to voice something that would have been unimaginable to him even a few hours ago.

'It was this photo of us from tonight,' he said eventually. 'The way you're looking at me. I saw it. The love in your eyes. I understand now. You love me, like Elisabetha loved her prince.'

Violetta's eyes glittered with moisture as she turned to place a kiss in his palm. 'Always, Leo. Always and for ever.'

He rolled her onto her back. 'Always,' he echoed, pressing a tender kiss to her lips. 'Always and for ever, my love.'

EPILOGUE

LEO WAS THE last to retire, putting off the lights in the kitchens as he went.

He passed the dining room, where the table was already laid with crisp linens. Crystal champagne flutes sparkled amongst all the evergreens and icy-white baubles that Francesca and Luisa had spent the afternoon gathering and arranging in displays along its centre.

Tomorrow they'd have a lavish Christmas Day dinner, with everyone dressed to the nines. But to-night his guests had shared an informal and often raucous meal, gathered round the oak table in the kitchen. The servants had been given time off to celebrate with their own families and Violetta and Matteo had stepped in as cooks, serving up home-made pasta with Grand-Mère's famous pomodoro sauce, followed by tiramisu from Matteo's closely guarded recipe.

The kitchen had echoed to the laughter and teasing of his oddball gathered family. Leo had sat at the head of the table, surveying the scene in some wonder.

Previously estranged sisters, a former fiancée and the man she'd jilted Leo for.

Max was there, with his new fiancé. A wildly handsome major from the Grimentzian Guards who'd seen something lovable in the previously unlovable Max and helped him reveal it to the rest of the family.

Believing he might now be freed of the terrifying responsibility of being the sole heir, Max had abandoned his dissolute lifestyle. His major had encouraged him to face his demons and find a new purpose in life.

Leo knew they'd never be close as he and Seb were, but Max was still family and Violetta had taught him how important it was to cherish those bonds. He'd witnessed how she'd pulled her sister close and how much that relationship meant to her now.

So Leo had made the first move by asking his cousin if he could take on the patronage of a new charity that helped young people with mental health issues and Max had actually agreed.

Inviting him to spend Christmas here at the chateau had also felt right and seeing him that evening talking with Seb, almost like the brothers they were, had pleased Leo beyond all measure.

Earlier that day the brothers, the major and Francesca's husband had been tasked by Violetta with dressing the enormous tree that occupied a corner of the hallway.

The men had discharged their duties with gusto. Hardly an inch was bare of decoration. Grand-Mère would have loved how ostentatious it was.

She would have loved even more how Leo had gathered his new family around him for Christmas.

You were happy here once, she'd written. *You could be again.*

She was right. He was…almost. Something niggled at him. Something about Violetta this evening that he couldn't quite put his finger on.

Because his happiness was, of course, inextricably linked with hers.

A toy tractor dangled from a branch just above his head. Violetta's little nephew had been transfixed by it. Importuning 'Unca Lo' again and again to lift him up on his shoulders so he could inspect it more closely.

Leo wondered when he might do the same with a son—or daughter—of his own. He knew he just needed to be patient. He and Violetta would have children in time. They certainly weren't childless for want of trying.

His sigh was answered by the tap of four paws trotting close and a wet snout shoved into his hand.

Leo fussed at soft ears then crossed the hallway to climb the stairs to join his wife in their bedroom.

The hound had joined the family some months back. Carrying on Grand-Mère's tradition, he was a rescue dog.

A three-year-old Newfoundland-Malamute cross called Hektor.

Leo reached the landing. But the big dog was no longer following.

Hektor had halted next to the room occupied by the chateau's smallest guest. Torn between loyalty to Leo and his new-found adoration of Francesca's tiny son, he gave a frustrated whine.

'It's okay, boy,' Leo said and Hektor sank to the rug. As if to cement his decision, he lay down blocking the way. To reach any of the rooms along the corridor an intruder would now have to go past him first.

'That's a good compromise,' Leo said. Hektor's tail thumped against the floor in agreement.

Francesca's son was to be well protected tonight.

Leo carried on, past the room that had temporarily become a nursery.

Any child of theirs would potentially become Head of State for both countries, but no child of his would suffer the emotional neglect and cruelty that he and Violetta had. There'd be no expectations other than they be themselves and if a younger child wanted the role and the eldest did not, then that would be up for discussion also.

Their offspring would never suffer the loveless lives their parents had. He and his wife had a loving family around them now, as would their children.

Wife.

Leo still couldn't get used to how wondrous that was to him.

She was wife and lover first, his consort second. How she'd helped him in those last stages of rebuilding Grimentz.

When he entered their room Violetta was at the window with the curtains drawn back.

'Look,' she said, 'it's snowing.' She came towards him, her eyes alight with excitement.

In the distance the bells of St Peter's cathedral and all the churches of Grimentz rang out for midnight.

'It's Christmas,' Violetta said. In her ivory nightgown she looked like his bride all over again. His breath caught in his throat. He still hadn't got used to the physical impact she could have on him. He doubted he ever would and he didn't want to.

However much it scared him, how much his love for her filled his soul, he wouldn't trade even a moment of it for what he'd had before.

A grey, cold and loveless half-life.

At first there had been days when the old fears had come crashing back and he'd faltered and hidden away. But Violetta had always found him, wound her arms about his neck, held him, kissed him, reassured him.

It was okay to be scared, she'd told him, she was too. Then she'd remind him they'd get through this together and each day it got easier and better and loving her became the most natural and important thing he could do.

Because she was his love.

Right now, with her slender body pressed against him, her eyes bright with excitement, she was up to something. He knew that look well.

'I know we're supposed to be exchanging gifts in the morning, but now it's officially Christmas I want to give you something tonight.'

He glanced around for a surprise parcel, wrapped in festive paper, adorned with a bow perhaps. But there was nothing.

Instead she took his hand, gently spreading his fingers to open his palm. She pressed a kiss to it, turned it and carried it downwards to lay flat against her belly.

His long fingers easily encompassed her and... and...

Leo's heart stuttered. Now he knew what he'd missed at dinner. She'd passed on the wine and drunk water all evening.

His gaze shot to hers to find it brimming with love.

'Yes, Leo.' She smiled at him then. 'I'm pregnant. You're going to be a father.'

As his family slumbered and the snow softly fell and the church bells rang out for a bright, new

Christmas morning, Leo gathered his wife and unborn child to him.

Happiness, he thought. *This is how it feels.*

* * * * *

If you loved the drama in
Stranded with His Runaway Bride
make sure to catch up on Julieanne Howells's debut for Harlequin Presents
Desert Prince's Defiant Bride *Available now!*